I0631369

Summer Holidays

Koral Dasgupta doesn't create stories—they happen to her. She processes them into her books, academic lectures, speeches, columns and paintings. Other than writing books, teaching management and speaking assignments, she works on her dream venture, www.tellmeyourstory.in

Summer Holidays is her fourth book. Her other three books are *Power of a Common Man, Fall Winter Collections* and *Rasia: The Dance of Desire*.

She can be reached on the Twitter handle @KoralDasgupta

Summer Holidays

Koral Dasgupta

RUPA

Published by
Rupa Publications India Pvt. Ltd 2019
7/16, Ansari Road, Daryaganj
New Delhi 110002

Sales Centres:
Allahabad Bengaluru Chennai
Hyderabad Jaipur Kathmandu
Kolkata Mumbai

ISBN: 978-93-5333-376-8

First impression 2019

10 9 8 7 6 5 4 3 2 1

The moral right of the author has been asserted.

To my cousins, who make life a laugh riot.
And to my son, Neev, who makes up for it
when they aren't around.

Prelude

2001

'Shiraaaaaaz!'

The shrill cry of his tender voice rent the calm of those last traces of darkness. The gardener left his pruner to look up at the balcony, surprised. A broad smile lit up the little face. That innate happiness of the child on spotting the older man was heart-melting. The gardener quickly raised his hand to greet him, but his innocent excitement had already woken up the rest of the house. They were now desperately trying to pull him inside, so he could be wrapped in warmer clothes. Soon he was back inside the cozy walls. But his steady wails continued to reject the secure comfort, as the colours of dawn slowly nudged at the lethargic eastern sky. The gardener knelt on the ground to pray.

As the first of the sun's rays fell on the valley, Saundarya, the babysitter, led the children to the garden, as she always did during their holidays. The little ones soon busied themselves with running after butterflies and grasshoppers, amid marigolds, sunflowers, daisies and lilies. She quietly disappeared into the kitchen to make some dosa for herself. She never could understand why these silly north Indians couldn't put some tamarind or coconut in their food. What was the point of adding oodles of chilli powder to turn every curry red-hot spicy?

As she entered the kitchen, Sunny, the cook, made a face and moved away. He carried with him the chicken pieces he had been dressing for lunch. Saundarya almost puked. Right when she had taken up the job, she had made it clear to the widower Major that she would like to have access to the kitchen. Not everyone's recipes suited her strict vegetarian tastes. Major Anil Dhillon had had no objection to this simple condition, but this cook's ego was hurt.

'When the owner of the house can happily have the food I cook, why can't the maid?' he had once grunted.

Saundarya had felt like punching him hard. 'I am not supposed to eat food prepared by those from the lower castes,' she had said, throwing on an air of superiority, satisfied with her revenge for having been called a maid. The funny-eyed cook fumed, but proved to be a hard nut to crack. Every day when it was her time to enter the kitchen, he would either be cleaning fish or roasting mutton or marinating chicken, making Saundarya, with her staunch Tamil Brahmin roots, feel violated. She would mutter a curse, sprinkle water around with her hands and say a small prayer seeking forgiveness for putting up with such uncultured behaviour. She needed the money to sustain herself, and the Major was paying well.

But that wasn't the only reason she was there. She loved the two kids, whose smiles and mischief lit up her day, and also the old lady, the Major's mother-in-law, called Nani by everyone. Quickly Saundarya prepared her sada dosas, put them on a porcelain plate, picked up a few tissues and headed out to the garden, back to the kids. There they were at the rear end, watching Shiraz work on the marigolds. She passed a dosa to the gardener, and took small bites from her own, simultaneously feeding the kids, who loved her simple cooking.

The morning was beautiful and serene. Major Dhillon's ancestral house on Raj Bhawan Road, Shimla, was active in the summers, when he came there for his holidays. Deepti, his sister, and her son, Rishi, also joined them. The Major wanted all of them to shift to Delhi, especially for the days he was on duty, but Nani wouldn't leave the house to caretakers. This was where her only daughter had breathed her last, after she had lost her bitter and brief battle with cancer. Every time Major Dhillon tried to explain to Nani that she and his daughter, Mira, would be safer and more accessible if they moved to Delhi, her throat would turn dry. 'Whoever wants to leave can go, but not me,' Nani would say.

Her helpless tears forced the Major to accede. But he ensured that the bungalow had tight security and the staff was extremely alert with visitors. Not that there was any potential threat. Everyone around the place knew the Dhillons. They were very old inhabitants. Even the cook, the gardener and the house help had been with the family for a long time—their parents had served the Major's father when he was alive. Relationships were deep, inherited and trustworthy. Only Saundarya was new. She had joined during the last days of Mira's mother. The lady had made Saundarya promise that she would never let her daughter feel she did not have a mother. And Saundarya had not failed her.

As she now made her way back to the kitchen to put her plate in the sink, she heard Major Dhillon arguing with his sister again in the room upstairs. They argued whenever they were together, over things that were frivolous and entirely avoidable. 'What kind of woman raises her voice so much while talking to her brother? Good women are always soft-spoken and devoted to the men in the family.' She grimaced at the boorish practices of the house, but then, who was she to question her employer's sister? She directed her displeasure at Sunny instead, who stood wide-eyed near the kitchen door, trying his best to catch every word.

'Get back to your work, hopeless creature!' Saundarya said in exasperation.

'Keep quiet, filthy woman,' Sunny retaliated. 'It is always important to keep your eyes and ears open. That's how you manage the pulse of a place and have its people in your grip.' He raised his hand, opened his palm and closed his fist to illustrate the point. Saundarya turned away in distaste and closed her eyes for a prayer, hoping that the offensive cook would vanish and the Major's sister would gain some temperamental transformation.

Deepti and Rishi had reached Shimla two days back. Mira, a usually quiet girl, was at her happiest when she was with Rishi. The two would always be up to something, thinking of ways to break the mundane quiet of the place.

Mira's reserve bothered Saundarya. The 7-year-old kid often stayed absorbed in a web of silence, making Saundarya feel that she hadn't been able to engage her well. The girl had lost her mother three years back, but she was too young to realize what had gone from her life. And the child responded with a strange detachment from life itself.

With Rishi, Mira got back the mirth and naughtiness of a normal 7-year-old. Maybe because Rishi, two years younger than her, didn't give in to her melancholic bouts. He dragged her along into things he wanted to do—and Mira let him, happily going along with his whimsical ideas. She also loved her bua. She loved to sleep cuddled with her aunt. Deepti's bedtime stories took her to the world of palaces and princes, their chivalrous deeds and heroic wins. Rishi would listen to the stories patiently, and then complain they were too girly, irking both his mother and cousin. Sometimes they sat with Nani, and the old woman narrated to them tales from the epics. With Rishi and Deepti, Mira was never pensive. And Saundarya was grateful to Deepti for that.

Now, as she sat watching the kids play in the garden, loud and sharp voices tore at the calm of the morning! Puzzled and scared, the kids ran towards Saundarya, but their babysitter was just as confused. Slowly, unsure of what might follow, she led the kids towards the bungalow. They took quiet steps into the sitting area, where Sunny stood terrified, his eyes fixed on the room upstairs that opened next to the stairs. Saundarya and the kids looked on while Nani's feeble voice from inside the room kept asking what the commotion was all about. No one had the courage to move.

The Major and his sister were still at it. The house had witnessed their disagreements and anger before. But never at this level, at this pace and for so long! Both brother and sister were strong-headed and stubborn, unrelenting to anything that did not have their approval. Today their differences seemed to have come to a head.

'Someone stop them,' Nani called out. Before Saundarya could figure out what to do, the door upstairs burst open. Deepti stormed out and strode into the room she occupied with Rishi. She emerged a few minutes later with her bags packed,

ready to leave. Without looking at anyone, she ordered a cab
to be summoned. The command was followed immediately. She
did not even wait for Rishi to change; nor did she bid goodbye
to those who stood watching her in shock. After she had loaded
her luggage into the cab, she looked down at Mira, holding
on to a corner of her sari with weak, trembling fingers, tears
streaming down her little face. Deepti knelt down in front of
the little girl, hugged her tight, kissed her forehead and asked
her to be taken away. She pulled Rishi into the cab, despite his
vehement protests—and they were gone!

Unable to understand why her bua had left with her cousin
so abruptly, Mira ran upstairs to her father. But she stopped at
the door. Dense smoke from her father's pipe filled the room.
He was standing by the window, eyes fixed on something
outside, but looking at nothing. Even at that tender age, Mira
sensed that something had gone irreversibly wrong. And quietly,
as she always did, she walked away.

1.

'She's watching you.'

Rishi's friend Vidit, nicknamed Poncho for the generous belly he had given himself, forced his sleepy eyes open. Rishi's words conjured up vague images in his drowsy brain. Who was watching? The cool trainee at his father's office? The pretty schoolmate who cried on his shoulder every time she broke up? Her suspicious mother? The attractive classmate? The newly joined cutie in first year? The lady constable who had fined him in the morning for taking a wrong turn? The journalist from Indian TV who shouted at anyone she talked to? Who?

Still groggy, he turned to Rishi for clarification. His friend pointed to the old sweeper mopping the balcony outside their classroom.

'What nonsense!' Poncho grumbled a little too loudly, his anticipations falling flat. He was about to give his friend an earful for interrupting his well-strategized nap in the corner of the classroom, when a meek voice called out his name.

'Excuse me, gentleman, what's cooking there?'

Professor Arunava Mukherjee never looked at the offender, perhaps worried he'd not be able to reprimand them if they seemed too repentant. Poncho frowned at Rishi, apologized to the professor, excused himself to splash some water on his face—and didn't return for the rest of the class.

Rishi and Poncho were students of Indian Academy of Design (IAD) in Mumbai. The design and fashion institute stood in stark contrast to the crowd and traffic of Andheri, like a snobbish, glamorous diva distanced from the suffocating hustle by the towering point of her stilettoes. Right at the orientation, the students were told that the institute valued ambition over dreams. Rishi knew exactly what it meant. But how such an institute could accommodate someone like Poncho was beyond him. And also Dr Arunava Mukherjee. The little hair he had, all incidentally concentrated on the right side of his head, was carefully combed to cover the bald patch at the centre. The professor would often pat his head to check if the strands were still in place.

After class, it fell on Rishi to provide his classmates with some comic relief. He was the master of imitation—the canteen guy who never smiled, the sweeper who loved to talk, the classmates who hated each other, the boy who stood outside the campus secretly selling cigarettes and the watchman nicknamed Sanskari, who would chase him away—no one was spared. Everyone laughed and clapped as he rounded up the act with a flourish; some even demanded repeat performances of certain parts. Finally, after the gang dispersed, Rishi looked at the papers that lay on Poncho's desk. The ever-heartbroken lad had been attempting a love note again, before his passion fell victim to slumber.

'The spellings of "compassion" and "graceful" are wrong,' Rishi had pointed out last time.

'Is that all you see?' Poncho, sunk into the web of one-sided romance, had turned to rebuke him. 'Spelling, grammar and language! Look beyond, moron. You have a lover's heart there.'

Rishi had continued to look straight at the professor with a deadpan face, and Poncho had been thrown out for disturbing the class. On more than one occasion, he had spent the rest of the minutes in the college canteen or the library, trying to pack more praises into the letter, so that it wouldn't come back crumpled or torn, accompanied by verbal abuse, or worse still, with an aggressive gang of girls born to corner nice boys like him.

Like other times, Rishi joined him after class. But Poncho couldn't for the life of him comprehend what kept his friend glued to 90-minute monologues. When Rishi had joined IAD, no one took him seriously. Perceptions changed when this lanky boy, who looked at everyone as if they were a pack of jokers, suddenly scored better than the most promising students in class. Soon there was a reshuffling of interpersonal equations. The cream of the class suddenly wanted to ditch the front rows to sit with him. Neither Rishi nor Poncho appreciated this sudden gush of affection. One day at the canteen, Poncho had lashed out. 'You should have told me that you were so good with your submissions!'

Rishi took a huge bite of the sandwich and mumbled with his mouth full, 'Why, what would you have done? Copied?'

'No,' Poncho replied, 'I wouldn't have been your friend at all. I don't like the topper type. They are depressing. Ouch!'

Rishi had kicked him in the knee before he could finish. Poncho rubbed his leg and laughed.

The banter of the two friends was often interrupted by someone or the other from class, wanting to join in with a cuppa, speaking aimlessly for a while and then proposing that

Rishi partner with them in their project. Every time, Rishi would thank them and inform them that he had already partnered with Poncho. In a few hours, his cell phone would be full of messages with advice and warnings.

'You aren't making a wise choice.'

'Poncho will not add value to your work.'

'Why are you wasting yourself with that duffer?'

'What are you doing, man? Poncho doesn't even have a clear vision. What will he fetch a promising guy like you? Think, buddy.'

Rishi would just smile. Poncho was no go-getter; he was reluctant to take any initiative and chase it to completion. And that's exactly why he made a great partner for someone as ambitious as him. All his childish madness aside, Poncho was a fantastic executor and an acclaimed *jugaadu*. He could plead, beg, snatch, run or do anything to arrange for the stuff he required. No futile ego, no false pride. Rishi, on the other hand, was too high-headed for such antics. No one trusted him like Poncho did. Not just college, given a choice, he wouldn't let Poncho go his whole life.

Later that evening, Rishi's Honda CBR roared into the peaceful parking space in Powai. As he took off his helmet and locked the bike, the curtains of the room two floors above shifted, and the twin sisters peeped out. A smile touched his lips. An ultra-humid July night, a superbike and two interested women—what more could he ask for? He stayed put for a while, checking the bike from all sides, giving the twins, Mili and Lily—he almost cracked up at the rhyming names—a little more time to look. Then he turned, strode out of the parking space and took the stairs two at a time to reach the one-room apartment he had been able to afford in one of the most happening localities of Mumbai. Akshat Uncle, an old family friend, had helped him find it. Surprisingly, the rent was nominal. He was told that the NRI owner of the house didn't need money, just a trusted paying guest to keep an eye on his ageing mother. This mother stayed in the adjoining flat. Often, she would send across tasty snacks from her kitchen. Poncho suspected that she also had a single daughter, which would explain her soft corner for the tenant.

Rishi turned the key to open the door and grimaced. Seemed like the maid had bunked again. She probably didn't find much sense in cleaning a young bachelor's den every day. Rishi picked up some garbage lying on the floor and shoved it into the dustbin. After he had washed and changed, he entered the kitchen. There would not be freshly cooked food this evening. He cursed the maid, toasted some slices of bread and washed them down with water. It was only 9 p.m.—sleep was still a few hours away. Not yet full, he dug out a packet of popcorn stocked some donkey's years ago in a corner of his flat. Balancing the popcorn in one hand, he opened his laptop to find out what was happening on Facebook.

Lovely selfies. Perfect friendships. Philosophies of being. Travel updates from the Alps. Gorgeous, colourful lives all over. All so mindlessly boring! He picked up his shoes instead. The poor things were once black. Now they carried endless splotches and marks. He dug out a used brush and set to cleaning them, while simultaneously answering a few chats that came his way.

Just when he was about to shut down his laptop, the People You May Know section on the right caught his eye. He clicked on a profile.

Most of the data was hidden from unapproved visitors, but there was a profile image. Hair flowing wild, thick eyebrows, full lips, brown, dreamy eyes somewhat detached from the present, as they always used to be, the nose a little flat at the tip—something he had always poked fun at and gotten scolded by his mother as Mira sulked in a corner…

Mira! His cousin Mira! Why hadn't he looked for her earlier? These days everyone was on social media! A big smile appeared on his face, and he clicked on the Add Friend tab.

2.

'She should have gone for him. Her children and husband had no time for her. Is it worth giving up love for mundane responsibilities that aren't valued anyway?' The hibiscus tree in the garden swayed in support. But the tall neem tree looked down from afar, stern and rigid, as if questioning her. 'Would love have made her happy if it carried the burden of guilt?'

The Bridges of Madison County lay open on the table. The story went over and over in her head, arguments in favour of both love and responsibility vying to one-up the other. She fantacized about a Robert Kincaid opening his arms for her. 'I'd go,' she decided stubbornly. 'Who knows if there's anything like lifelong happiness? I'd choose short-term pleasure over searching endlessly and impractically for the joy of a lifetime.'

She shoved the book away and frowned at the neem tree. Her brain still questioned the morality of the imaginary decision. From the pile of books and notebooks arranged shape-wise on the table, she pulled out a diary. 'Problem No. 3,276: Responsibility vs Love,' she wrote. She slammed it shut, just as a ping on her laptop notified her of an update. Lazily, she pulled it to herself, and froze.

She had been a frequent visitor to his profile. Of course, he didn't know, but there seemed to be nothing private for this boy. All his updates were in the public domain and anyone could view what he put up on his timeline. She knew he had enrolled on an Applied Arts course. And that his relationship status read, 'It's complicated.' Many times she had been tempted to send him a friend request, or at least tell him about cyber safety. But every time she had stopped, lest her concern be read as interference.

'Why didn't Rishi come back? Why did Deepti Bua take him away just because she had had a fight with dad? Why can't dad just forgive and forget?' she had often asked herself. Many times Mira had even walked up to her father, a Major General now, to tell him that she wanted to meet Rishi again. Halfway down the path she always came back without a word, because it felt that the hurt in her father's heart was way deeper than hers. She couldn't stop herself from peeping into Rishi's Facebook profile, though, taking in every available detail. He was always surrounded by friends and had all kinds of people posting on his wall, wishing him something or the other, tagging him in photographs or commenting on his statuses.

Only Mira was left alone.

Slowly, as if making sure that no one was watching, Mira accepted the friend request. A chat box popped open almost immediately, prompting her to answer the video call.

'Popcorn or ice cream?'

Mira smiled. The same old out-of-context nonsense. 'Popcorn,' she said.

'Here, have some!' Rishi threw some popcorn at the webcam. He laughed.

Mira laughed too. 'What if I had said ice cream? Would you have smeared ice cream on your computer?'

'No, silly! I'd just say go buy one from the parlour. How's you, Browny?'

Rishi had always called her Browny because of her brown eyes. He had often sat in front of her, looking at her eyes with a frown, trying to understand why they were different from his black ones. Mira had been longing to hear him call her that again, but she just feigned scorn, just as she had when she was a kid.

'Don't call me Browny!' she retorted. Rishi laughed again. 'How is Shiraz?'

Shiraz! The first person Rishi recalled from Shimla was Shiraz! Mira buried the question in her heart. 'How are you?' she asked instead.

'Just as you see.' Rishi shrugged. 'What's happening with Major Sahab?' he asked, adding hastily, 'Hey, forget Major Sahab—how's Sunny? Does he still prepare those chicken balls and chaats at home?'

'Yes, he still does.' And she held up the plate of basil chicken she had been eating.

Rishi let out a cry of disappointment. 'Don't do this to me, you sick little Browny! Here I am, having popcorn because the maid bunked, and there you are, showing me Sunny's basil chicken!'

He fell back, resigned, on the large bean bag. Mira swayed a piece of chicken enticingly in front of the camera and shoved it inside her mouth.

'Here, I'm having it on your behalf. Feel the taste.' She closed her eyes, munching in satisfaction. She could almost hear him cursing from the other side. She opened her eyes and chuckled.

'Why didn't you ever come back?' she asked hesitantly.

Soft melancholy tinged the ever-happy face. 'Things are

bad, Mira. Mom suffers in silence. She's too stubborn to take that step forward. Dad tries to talk to her, but she won't. What would I say to mama or mom, if I were to go to your place? No point complicating things.'

Mira agreed. 'Dad, too, misses bua, and you. I have seen him going through the old albums when no one is around. But he refuses to talk about it. This brother-sister duo is just too strange and difficult.' She looked sad.

'Forget it,' Rishi tried to brush the subject aside. 'How's Saundarya Ma?'

'Don't ask.' Mira made a face. 'She's throwing a fit because I'm leaving home for higher studies. She is wailing, shouting, pleading and sulking around the house.'

'These women, I tell you,' laughed Rishi. 'Mom almost did the same when I left home. When I boarded the flight, I had a red tika on my forehead, a home-made cake and a box of biryani packed in my luggage.'

They both laughed, trying to imagine what the other's life would have been like all these years. And suddenly, both spoke together.

Rishi's 'Where are you going?' came at the same time as Mira's 'Let's catch up next month'. They paused, their breathing quickening in anticipation, and both uttered together: 'Mumbai!'

Neither cousin knew whether it was excitement, shock or happiness, but both stared at each other for a good fifteen seconds without a word. It was Rishi who broke the silence.

'When?'

'14th,' Mira's mouth had gone dry. 'Powai...M.Tech... IIT Bombay.'

Rishi snapped his fingers. 'Come and put up with me,

Browny. Withdraw your hostel applications in secret; make sure no one accompanies you to Mumbai. That way, they'll not know that we got in touch, and we can stay together.'

Mira hit the screen with the palm of her hand in a high five. 'I'll do that! Dad keeps saying I need to take care of stuff by myself. He feels I am too dependent on Saundarya Ma. I'll use his words against him to crack this.'

They talked for some more time, exchanged numbers, pulled each other's leg and logged off. Neither could sleep that night.

The days that followed seemed to go too slowly for Mira. Major General Dhillon was surprised by his daughter's sudden enthusiasm to move to Mumbai. Usually she got teary-eyed every time Saundarya wailed.

'Aren't there enough colleges around here to admit a talented child?' Saundarya would ask. Or she would grumble, making sure the Major was within earshot. 'Women do not need too much education. We should rather get her married, so I can move in with her to take care of her new house and the children, when Mira has her own! But who will listen to me?'

Mira just laughed her concerns off and assured her that she would take her Saundarya Ma with her when she got a job. Happy that his daughter was finally outgrowing her introverted nature, the Major seemed relieved, much to the wrath of Saundarya.

'Don't blame me if the girl gets out of hand,' she muttered angrily.

A few days before Mira had to take the train to Mumbai,

she instructed Sunny to pack some of his best culinary offerings for her, surprising the two men and the woman of the house. No one had ever thought that Mira had favourites. She had never expressed her opinion, either in favour of or against anything. Choices led to conversations, so she avoided the hassle and settled for the more reassuring silence.

Sunny, a man in his forty-sixth year now, with a receding hairline but attitude as aggressive as always towards things he disliked, was elated, though. He went around telling everyone that Mira Baby had asked him to pack her 'favourite dishes'.

Soon the time came to bid adieu. A tearful Sunny and Saundarya saw her off at the front gate of their house. Mira hugged them tight till her father's car honked loudly. As the car drove through the open roads of Saharanpur, she looked at her father. The grey had spread generously through his once-jet-black hair. He had shifted to the Army quarters of Saharanpur ten years back, after Nani breathed her last. Surprising herself and shocking her father, Mira asked what had often crossed her mind but she had never dared to utter. 'Dad, why didn't you marry again after mom left us?'

Major General Dhillon turned to look at his daughter, trying to gauge where this was coming from. But all he did was give her a stern frown.

'Not all stepmoms are wicked, you know.' Mira nudged him, as softly as she could. 'You need a companion. Aren't you lonely otherwise? See, even I am leaving...' Her voice tightened. Now her father smiled, assured that this was a daughter's concern for leaving her father behind. A pensive look clouded his face as he stared outside the window.

'I have never been good with relationships, Mira.' He took

a deep breath. 'I am responsible, I can provide, I can ensure that a routine doesn't ever fail. But most of the times, I don't understand, or share, or care. If your mother was alive today, she wouldn't have been a happy woman.' He smiled sadly.

Mira felt a lump in her throat. Her father had never talked like this. 'That's not true, Dad. You have kept me happy, even without a mother; why wouldn't anyone else be?' Her father affectionately touched her head. 'You are not happy either, Mira. You just didn't ever demand a change.'

A few hours later, the train at the station hooted, signalling it was time for departure. As it started moving, and the tall figure of her father receded, Mira wished there was another way to make all this work. A gnawing sadness battled optimistic excitement inside her as every turn of the wheel took her towards Rishi. It was the start of a new life.

3.

Three assignments back to back. Submission dates had suddenly been announced. The computer lab was abuzz with creative activity. Ambitious, restless brains worked overtime to get things done. A million improvisations, running to the faculty to consult on projects, and then applying their advice and technical interpretations had left Rishi exhausted. Back to his flat, he unbolted the door mechanically and wanted to drop himself into a luxurious bathtub, surrounded by the calming comfort of warm water and scented candles. But, of course, the one-room-kitchen wasn't tailored to such fantasies.

Either he could go for a bath in that tiny washroom where he couldn't even stand with his arms outstretched, or he could simply hit the bed. Before he could decide, Rishi found himself plonking down on the bed. He placed a hand over his eyes to block the light. In Bollywood films, actors were prone to dramatically switching the bedside lamps on and off when tense. Apart from lighting up their best features in profile shots, the exercise seemed to calm them down. In the absence of a bedside lamp, Rishi reached into his pocket and dug out a matchbox. Well, some films did matchboxes too.

The first stick burnt out till the end, singeing his fingers. He threw it on the floor. He lighted the second and suddenly went blank. What time was it? A gentle press of the power button on his mobile phone told him it was 7.30 p.m. already.

Shit!

He would have to be at Bandra station at 9 p.m. to pick up Mira. He looked around. The room was a mess. Quickly he gathered the empty cigarette packets from the table and threw them into the dustbin. Empty wine bottles lying in the corners of the kitchen were packed into a plastic bag and dumped outside, near the stairs. He tried his best to put the books, newspapers and magazines in order. He discovered a shoe rack lying neglected at the entrance and neatly arranged all his shoes and slippers there. Finally, he straightened out the bedcover. It covered less than the length of his mattress. He tried to adjust it as best he could and looked around. The room looked different, clean. He smiled. Lowering his head towards his chest, he sniffed. Boy, working blood and sweat through assignments brought body odour as reward! Within the next few seconds, he used ample deodorant, changed his shirt and dashed out.

Rishi ran through the platform like a lunatic. The train had reached about seven minutes back. There she stood, peeping out of a compartment. Rishi slowed down, overpowered by a surge of emotions. Mira, with those hazelnut brown eyes and hair neatly tied, looked around for him, scanning the crowd on the platform. For a few seconds, he just stood there, watching her. And then he began running again.

'Mira!' he called out.

Mira smiled in relief and jumped down to the platform. Rishi reached out to hug her but she pushed him aside. 'Get the luggage down first, duffer. You are late already. I don't want my luggage going all the way to Hyderabad with this train.'

He followed Mira's finger to the luggage waiting to be

hauled off the compartment. They caught hold of the bags together and dragged them down one by one. As soon as the last bag hit the ground, the guard blew his whistle. Rishi looked at them and then at Mira. Two large suitcases, one huge bag, one backpack, one laptop bag and one sling bag. Mira was watching his irritation with unmasked glee on her face. She stopped him before he could open his mouth. 'One of these has Sunny's basil chicken. Say a word and you aren't getting it.'

Rishi's face changed immediately. 'Wicked!' he muttered and started arranging the luggage so they could pull them to the exit.

The cabbie threw a fit. He demanded an escalated fare for packing so many bags on top. A few arguments later, they drove off.

'Madam in Mumbai for first time?' he asked, wiping sweat off his forehead with a dirty piece of cloth.

Rishi spoke before Mira could. 'How do you know it's Madam who has come to Mumbai and not me?'

The driver smiled sarcastically—the kind when one knows the other has asked a silly question. 'No man carries this much luggage, Sir.'

Rishi looked at Mira; she frowned.

'So which place are you from?' the cabbie asked again.

'Delhi.' Mira was curt.

'Where in *Dilli*?' The guy showed no signs of interpreting her body language. 'People who stay 100 km from *Dilli* also say they are from *Dilli*!' He looked through the rear-view mirror and saw Mira getting furious; it only seemed to egg him on.

'Ghaziabad is Dilli. Agra, Mathura is Dilli. Sometimes even Benaras is Dilli. Ha ha ha!'

Mira tightened her fingers into a fist, but the man was not done yet. 'So many bags, on top of that. Either madam is running away from home or she comes from a small village in Haryana. People of these villages carry all their belongings when they come to big cities. Because they think that in big cities, everything is too expensive and everybody is a thug! Then they say they are coming from *Dilli*, to show off their status.' He grinned again.

Mira was on the verge of erupting, when Rishi called out, 'Hey, here! Stop the car.'

Confused, both Mira and the cabbie looked at him. The vehicle came to a screeching halt at the side of the road. He stepped out and made as if to unstrap the bags.

'But you said you were going to Powai?' the cabbie asked, astonished.

'Eight kilometres from Powai is also Powai. We are people from a small village in Haryana. And,' he paused, 'when the fair is ₹500, we pay only ₹150. Small-town syndrome, you see.'

'Come out Mira, quick,' he added.

It took both of them a few seconds to understand what Rishi was doing. Mira burst out laughing; the cab driver scratched his head and smiled gingerly. 'Sit in the cab, Sir. What jokes you rich men crack at poor people like us...!' He emptied a packet of foul-smelling gutkha into his mouth and starting the engine again. This time the *kali-peeli* drove fast, and in silence—only the muffled sound of the cousins giggling in the rear seat was audible.

✻

Home, finally.

Rishi unloaded the suitcases and dropped them in the portico of the society. Turning to Mira, he held her by the arm. 'Come, I'll introduce you to someone.'

'Now? I haven't yet changed. I need to take a bath first. I must change out of these stinking clothes that smell of everyone I was sitting with in that train,' Mira shrieked. But Rishi was already dragging her to the garage.

'Meet Virat Kohli,' he said, patting the seat of his bike proudly.

He turned to find Mira looking at him incredulously, hands on her waist. She looked at the bike and back at her cousin.

'Virat Kohli!' she exclaimed.

'Oh, yes. He's a champ. You just have to hear him roar. Come, try him. Let's go for a spin. Don't worry about your stupid Haryanvi luggage. No one will touch them. Even thieves in Mumbai have finer taste.' He gestured to Mira to take the pillion seat. Mira slapped him on the shoulder.

'Take me to your room, moron. I am tired. I need to take a bath and unpack before I crash.'

Rishi grew pale. 'You plan to unpack before you sleep?' The image of an overstuffed wardrobe cropped up before him. He had forgotten to make space for Mira. If only he could delay that. Not now! He needed to sleep too. But his expectations were crushed.

'Yes, I can't sleep till I have settled in. Now, can we go upstairs?'

Rishi tried to detract her for some time, before finally giving in. They entered the room. Mira looked around. Her expression made it all too clear that she wasn't impressed. In one corner a wrought-iron bed screamed for attention, as one end of the cover hung like a royal lady's gown while the other side of the bed starved for it. The brother had placed the longer side of the cover along the breadth of the bed. Without a word, she pushed him aside and set the bedcover straight, matching its length and breadth properly. She looked up to realize that Rishi was least bothered about the bedcover. Rather, he was staring strangely at the wardrobe.

She took a quick bath and started zipping open her suitcases. They disposed of the dinner prepared by Rishi's maid to binge on Sunny's delicacies. Soon Rishi was lying flat on the bed. He hid his face with a pillow, warning Mira for the last time. 'Think again. Your stuff won't rot if they are in the suitcase for another night. Tomorrow we can together...'

She cut him short. 'Go off to sleep, dumb; I will...OUCH!'

With a loud thump Mira fell back on the floor, with the wardrobe flung open. A pile of clothes had tumbled out and lay scattered around her.

'Duffer!' she shouted, removing creased shirts from her shoulder and her lap. 'Is this the way to keep things?'

'I did warn you...' Rishi moved the pillow from his face to look at her, laughed and went off to sleep.

4.

After neatly arranging her cousin's clothes and hers in separate chambers of the wardrobe and cleaning the room sufficiently, Mira was ready to hit the bed. It was almost morning. The brother lay like a king, his legs sprawled and arms at a weird angle. She caught his legs and pushed them to one side. Rishi didn't even realize that he had been moved. Mira tucked herself in towards the wall, trying not to occupy much space. With a thin sheet she covered herself from head to toe and lost herself in a deep sleep.

When the Mumbai sun shone on her face through the bed sheet, she removed the thin sheet and looked around. Rishi was at the window, trying to capture something with his DSLR. Must be a beautiful bird. She got up, walking quietly to stand behind him.

There was a slum outside. People were taking turns to enter a common toilet with a tin door. Those waiting their turn were either shouting at the person inside or banging on the door from outside. The thin sheet of tin threatened to give way, but that didn't seem to bother anyone. Finally, a man came out adjusting his lungi, cursing furiously and kicking at the line of people. The queue went berserk. Taking advantage of the commotion, a thin man saw his chance and slipped into the toilet, bolting the door. Immediately, the others went back to hurling abuses, complaining that the queue had been breached.

Astonished, Mira looked at Rishi. He was focused on these people fighting, laughing and making a complete mess of the beautiful morning. He clicked randomly, checking his shots on the camera and concentrating on the queue again.

'Ewwwww!' Mira couldn't hold it back any longer. Rishi looked at her, startled. 'How can you be so interested in a bunch of people waiting outside a public toilet? Sick!'

He chuckled. 'Emotions, my dear sis. They don't appear so conveniently in plush high-rise buildings. They come rugged and raw with the resourceless.' Rishi took out the data card and got busy fitting it into the laptop. Mira made a face.

'I haven't ever heard a more stupid philosophy. Early in the morning someone is busy capturing people fighting over a toilet!'

Rishi did not answer. Somewhat surprised by his silence, Mira bent forward to take a look at the screen open on his laptop. She didn't know the brother who would keep quiet at her potshots. What was wrong with this funny guy who always had a comeback? The images open on his screen did not show the toilet. Only the men in their colourful shorts, lungis and ganjees, either laughing, or looking on angrily, or saying something animatedly. The photographs spoke a different language—the language of energy, of vehemence, of chaos, connecting one human being with another. The language of life.

Not ready to admit so soon that the photos were really pretty good, she tried to keep the conversation going. 'So photography is a hobby?'

'No,' Rishi said without looking at her. He had started up a software on his laptop. 'It's life.'

The laptop hummed softly as the photographs were

imprinted with a 'Rishi Bahl' watermark at the bottom in a nice cursive font. He had done something to tone the photographs, adding some lustre and dimension through light and shade. Finished in greyscale, they now looked miraculously real, just scooped out from the morning some half an hour ago.

'You want a career in photography? Why are you doing this Communications Design course then?' Mira could not stop herself from asking.

'Graphics.'

The one-word response didn't make much sense to Mira.

'But shouldn't you do some short course on photography or at least intern with someone?'

The scepticism in her voice made Rishi turn. 'Do you know what graphics is? Or this communications design thing?'

Mira shook her head. 'No.'

He smiled. 'What do you think I should do with a degree in Applied Arts? What is the difference between fine art and applied art? What are the career options I have?'

The array of questions left Mira fumbling. 'Drawing teacher in a school?' she almost blurted out, but something in Rishi's eyes spelt sarcasm, and she numbed. *Something in films? Or fashion photography, maybe? Okay, fine, he could join the media. But fine art! Applied art! Well...!*

A loud snap interrupted her thoughts. Rishi had just pressed the shutter. She ran towards him in protest, relieved that the pointed questions had finally ended. He stopped her at an arm's length and turned the screen towards her. It showed a bewildered girl nervously trying to crack a code.

'Mom and dad have the same reaction when I try to talk to them about my career. They have no idea what I'm doing, and they won't listen even if I explain. They think I am wasting money.' He wiped the camera clean and placed it carefully back inside his box. Mira's next words made him turn sharply.

'Why can't you enrol on an academic course? You can pursue both together and see where that takes you.'

Rishi stood still. When he finally spoke, it seemed he was struggling to keep his tone neutral.

'Communications Design is an academic course, Browny. It is the graduate level. Training under it takes four years, the same as your B.Tech.'

Mira started feeling uncomfortable with her brother's sudden aggression. Perhaps Rishi sensed it too, and pulled back. But Mira had lost her zest. She had assumed that her cousin would always be as chilled out as he had been when they were kids. Now she was discovering this alien, sensitive side to him. She didn't know how to approach him or reassure him. Should she say sorry? No way, he would just use it to make fun of her later. Slowly, she tried again.

'I have seen all the stuff you put up on your social media. They're nice...'

'What you call *stuff* is my work, Browny.' Rishi looked like a rebel. 'My family doesn't understand that, and I have made peace with it.'

Mira paused for a while, took a deep breath and tried again.

'I am not a very ambitious person, you know,' she confessed. 'Just that I have taken seriously whatever I have done. I studied because that was the right thing to do. When grades were good, everyone said I must choose between a medical and an engineering career. I cracked engineering and got a job. But it felt terrible. Dad advised me to go back to academics. So I appeared for GATE and landed up here. After M.Tech, I will go for doctoral studies.' She looked at Rishi. 'I feel happy for you because you know what you want. I couldn't ever think beyond chasing the next obvious milestone.'

By then Rishi had relaxed. He was smiling.

'What?' asked Mira.

'A girl pursuing her M.Tech from IIT Bombay says she's not ambitious. And here I am, a student of Applied Arts at IAD, ambitious enough to look destiny in the eye and not blink till I win. We are irony personified, Browny.' He patted her on the head. The tension seemed to dissipate.

It was Mira's first day at IIT Bombay. They both had to rush. Rishi packed his bag and hers, dropping a set of duplicate keys into her bag before they left.

'You know how Kohli sends the ball soaring towards the boundary?' Rishi asked as they rode his bike. 'He stands erect as the ball comes from the front and swerves it towards the left like this.' As they approached a crossing, the red lights turned green and Rishi took a sharp turn towards the left, emulating the skipper's bat.

'Are you mad?' Mira cried. 'If you get caught by the traffic police, the BCCI won't be impressed.'

Rishi drove past the khaki-clad policeman standing a few metres away, writing something in a small pad in his hand. '...And here's the end of another over.' He stopped abruptly at the red signal, and his sister pushed him from behind, irritated.

When Rishi had dropped her off at IIT Bombay, Mira

turned towards her new college. There were the guest houses on the left, leading towards Powai Lake. For a moment, she forgot about the orientation she had to attend and walked mindlessly through the buildings, standing between two called Jal Vihar and Padma Vihar.

Not that she didn't know what an engineering college campus looked like. Her B.Tech days had neither been happening, nor boring. Just that everyone was a genius there. And everyone was in a hurry to prove that before the others. Competition was steep, teachers strict and schedules merciless. Most of the students there had a dream. Every project submitted was a reflection of that dream, which refused to shatter even when brutally criticized. But term exams were the levellers. The layers of pride and appreciation that the students wore as their second skin were ripped apart at the noticeboard that announced their results. Most of them had no idea what to say to their parents, who were waiting to hear that their child had topped! They would retire to the canteen discussing how engineering had ruined their lives. The flavourless tea poured into glasses carrying the smudged lip marks of the previous drinker felt far closer to their hearts than their choice of career.

The boy serving the tables tended to philosophize. 'All you buggers will become big people someday, and when you come to visit the campus, you will give me fat tips. Year after year I see students sitting here and lamenting. Then they go get themselves great jobs even before they've left the campus.'

Mira always felt the boy knew more about the campus than any of the professors or students. Listening to his rants were, in fact, quite therapeutic at the end of a hectic day. No more than 16, he carried with him the heart of the institute.

'Don't ever fall in love with anyone here, Mira Didi!' he would tell her. 'These people won't marry you. They just want a distraction from the academic grill. The lower their scores, the more their ego is bruised, the more their hatred for the teachers and the more praise they'll shower on you in their poetry. Don't ever believe you are as perfect as they say you are. You are just a temporary perfection in their lives as long as they are students here.'

The canteen owner would shout at him for spending too much time at the table, and he would run. But everyone knew there was no bigger entertainment than hearing his rants, which were both free and compulsory for everyone.

Mira missed him. He was the only one who actually seriously asked about her grades. He even scolded her when they were not up to the mark. Her father knew that Mira's interest in academics was pretty self-driven. She didn't have anything else to do other than study, and he didn't have to put in any effort in driving her. Saundarya Ma only asked if she had passed her exams. Every time she topped at school, Saundarya Ma would make a face. 'A woman studying so much, and also being a topper! God knows who will marry you.' She would grumble and then dramatically lower her voice. 'Men don't like women who are more intelligent than them. I mean, it's fine if you are more intelligent, but don't let it show.'

With such parenting samples back home, she would look forward to those affectionately stern queries at the canteen. The boy, too, had perhaps realized that this shy, timid woman didn't have friends.

Mira wished he was there that day; that he would suddenly appear from somewhere, shouting, 'Mira Didi, why are you standing here and wasting time? Your classes are about to begin. Run! Where are you lost?'

'Are you lost?'

The baritone came from behind. She turned, startled. A tall, young man was looking down at her from behind golden spectacles.

'No...er...I...' She tried to speak.

'Go straight. The academic building is on your right. The convocation hall is just opposite that,' he said, without shifting his gaze from her.

'Huh!' Mira was taken aback by the sudden directions this stranger was giving her. But the man looked even more surprised than her.

'Your orientation... You are already late and need to pace up to reach the convocation hall.' His voice was stern. It seemed to cut through her dreamy, memory-blessed morning.

'I...I am M.Tech,' she managed to say.

'Good for you, then; usually people come here to fetch that degree.'

'No,' she almost shouted. 'I am a first-year M.Tech student. Sorry.'

The man seemed to have given up on her. Wasting no more time, he nodded and walked on in long strides. Mira almost ran behind him.

God knew who he was! Why did he have to find her standing all alone like that, lost in some other world? What must he be thinking? Why couldn't he just disappear so she could run faster without looking like an ostrich galloping? He did finally disappear at one of the turns, and Mira ran into the convocation hall.

5.

'How was the first day at college, Browny?' Rishi asked on their way back.

'This hurts,' was all she said, trying to find a comfortable position on the pillion seat.

'Dumb!' snorted her brother. 'Any woman would give her right hand to be able to sit on Virat Kohli's lap.'

'Yes, she would. If he was for real and not an ill-metaphored Chinese torture,' she snarled back.

Rishi stopped abruptly. 'Get off my bike. Leave me alone with my Kohli.' He looked serious.

'I met this guy in college. Tall, fair, handsome. With almond-coloured skin,' she said.

'What!' Rishi took off his helmet and looked at her. 'Right on the first day of college you hooked someone? Who's he? Did he tell you anything? What's his name?'

Mira smiled calmly; she put the helmet back on his head as the light turned green and the vehicles around them started to honk. 'Let's go home first.'

All through the way, Rishi kept asking her about this almond-skin newcomer in their story. Mira kept ignoring him. From the hoarding above, Virat Kohli flaunted his designer kurta and trimmed beard. She winked at him as he disappeared at the next turn.

By the time they unlocked the door of their one-room flat, Rishi was at the very end of his patience. Mira burst out laughing.

'No, silly. I was walking too leisurely through the campus, looking at the greenery and thinking of my B.Tech days. Then there was this really tall, lean guy who reminded me that I was getting late and needed to rush to class. Nothing more.'

Rishi was still sceptical. 'Why did you talk about it?'

Mira chuckled. 'Just to distract you from your Kohli, duffer.' He frowned at her.

'Why do you call it Kohli?'

The frown was replaced with a smile. 'He is my star companion. We are brothers, you see. When everyone else abandons me, Kohli will still be there to encourage and inspire.'

She rolled her eyes. 'I hate cricket. Dad forgets life when there's a match.'

She looked at Rishi and her face lit up with a mischievous smile. She stretched. 'But he is handsome. I wish Virat Kohli wasn't a cricketer; maybe he could have been an engineer, you know, preferably in Communications.'

Dreamily she looked skywards and stood up dramatically on the bed. 'Just imagine, Virat Kohli is an IIT-IIM thing, working as the CEO of Intel. There he leads his team through technical innovations and defends them like a tiger. Every contract bowled to him turns out to be a chauka.' She gestured to indicate a boundary. 'A harder taskmaster than Steve Jobs, his media statements drenched in arrogance, his temperament a terror to competitors and his technical perfection dissected in B-School case studies. After every achievement, he throws a beach party where he dances around with...!'

Mira was already dancing away in the arms of Engineer Kohli on a starry night at the beach, when Rishi's voice jolted her back to their one-room apartment.

'Lizard, Browny! Watch out!'

Nearly jumping out of her skin, Mira yelped, lost her balance and crashed on the floor. Rishi was laughing hysterically. Mira slapped him hard on the leg. He cringed but continued laughing. He caught hold of his angry sister by the wrist, and pulled her up to sit next to him on the bed.

'Browny, do you have a boyfriend?' he asked, suddenly serious.

Mira was far from pleased with the prank, but she was even more surprised with the way her cousin switched moods. The seriousness on his face was disconcerting. This boy seemed to live life in nanoseconds, his emotions changing with the blink of an eye. She looked at him. He was waiting for an answer. She didn't understand Rishi when he was serious. She loved it when he laughed. It pulled her back into a happier time, when they were both kids and she waited for her brother to laugh and cheer up her world with his inherent happiness.

'No, I don't have a boyfriend,' she said. 'I never had one.'

'Really?' Rishi frowned. 'What were you doing during B.Tech? Only studying?'

Mira shrugged. 'Come to an engineering college sometime, you will know. There are just a handful of girls amid a bunch of men. Soon they are coming to you in slots, trying to befriend you and offering you cheap triple-boiled tea at the canteen. Later, when you are friends, they admit they are broke and you end up paying for all the filthy tea dates.'

Rishi smiled. 'So how many guys did you have cheap tea with?'

Mira smiled back and nudged him. 'You are interrogating me like my dad never did.'

'I know he didn't. That's why I am asking you. Come on, tell me, Browny. Any serious interest? Any secret crush?'

The smile faded. 'Nope. Beyond sharing my notes, no one quite found me interesting. All enthusiasm died when I chased them for work for group projects. Next project on, they enquired if there was a way to change teams.'

'And you?' Rishi probed.

Mira shook her head. She watched Rishi lie down on to the bed, staring at the ceiling.

'You have a girlfriend?' It was her turn to ask.

'No.'

'Then you have a boyfriend?' she smirked.

'Don't get smart.' He snapped at her, covering his eyes with his hand.

'This could not have been lying under the wardrobe because you treat it as home decor.'

Rishi jerked his head up. Mira was holding a pack of condoms in her hand. Quite unlike him, he was at a loss for words. The very next second, he sprang up and chased her around the room, trying to grab the pack.

'Tell me the truth, you pervert! Else I will take a snap of this and post it on your Facebook timeline,' she managed to gasp between squeals of laughter.

'None of your business,' he tried to say, but Mira had sensed gossip—she would not rest so easily. Rishi managed to corner her and force the packet out of her hands. He tossed it into the dustbin.

But Mira wouldn't give up. 'Are you telling me or not?

On Facebook your relationship status says "It's Complicated". I want to know who complicated your life. And how. Tell me right now, or else...!'

'You and your damned Facebook!' Rishi interrupted. 'That packet doesn't mean anything. Don't get ideas.'

Mira was looking at him like a teenager waiting to experience her first erotica. Eyes wide, she drew closer to him. 'You did it?'

Rishi burst into laughter. Mira joined him, wondering if the laughter meant a yes.

'No, dumb,' Rishi said, confusing her further. 'Actually, when I lived alone, there were all kinds of people who partied here. A lot of them were quite influential, with colourful tastes. Impression matters with people like them. To show them that I was not too different, I had to resort to some tricks. This was one of them.'

Mira was watching him in surprise. He tried to brush it off. 'You won't understand this, Browny. You don't need to.'

'But I want to,' Mira pleaded.

'Well,' Rishi turned to face her. 'I am trying to get into an industry where talent is in abundance, but it isn't measured in scores. Insecurity is high. We have to create our network, which must back us up. Some of the people I interact with don't hail from a background as humble as ours. These are important people with lots of money and contacts in their pockets. Many of them have wild, expensive fancies. A person who is different is considered a threat, because his tastes don't fall within the gamut of the tried and tested. And if he can't be comprehended, he gets isolated.'

He stopped to look at Mira again. She looked utterly

confused, trying to make sense of what Rishi had said. 'You might discover condoms and weed and such stuff in different corners of the house. I tried to clean it all before you came, but, of course, I may have missed some.' Mira's eyes had grown wide and there was a look of deep concern in them. Rishi pulled her hair. 'Don't try to judge me with those, Browny. I don't sleep around or smoke ganja or drink. When people came to my place, they left behind stuff. I didn't throw them away, so I could show them as mine. Clear now?'

Mira didn't know whether she should laugh or cry. Meekly, she asked, 'The relationship status on Facebook?'

'Oh, that?' Rishi smiled sheepishly. 'Actually, a "single" status sounds really boring. "It's Complicated", on the other hand, is more happening, though practically it's the same thing. I just made a wise choice.' He winked.

As Mira still looked on, he shrugged. 'It's actually quite cool to have cigarette packets and whisky bottles strewn around a bachelor's den, especially if he is an Art student. The first step to being a successful artist is to find a muse and name her as your inspiration. Later, it is either the inspiration or, in the absence of the inspiration, addiction, that helps you go far in this industry.'

Mira grimaced at the sarcasm. 'Nonsense!'

Rishi looked mischievous. 'What do you engineers do when frustrated? Drink rum? Or do rare nuts like you try to solve some tough mathematical graph to prove to yourself that life can be more difficult than the frustration at hand?'

'Shut up.' Mira's eyes narrowed in scorn.

Her brother sighed. 'It's true for us, Browny. How many in this world really bother about art? How many actually value it the way it should be? How many really respect an artist?' He stopped to drink water from a bottle, and looked back at her. 'The saddest status of artists in India is that you have to engage your audience with your personality more than with your work. Only Kohli can become Kohli overnight, if you know what I mean. The rest of the squad takes time.' He smiled.

'Why the hell do you bring Kohli into everything?'

'Because cricket is also art. Every day that hunk is performing a live show on the field. There are some like me who are floored by the way he treats the ball like his slave and the border like his den. And then there are some like you, who take care of the man on days he doesn't perform. On those days, his tattoos and his angry eyes do the trick, and he still earns from endorsements.'

'He doesn't have angry eyes. They are quite romantic, actually.' Mira looked at her brother. 'You know what, I think you are a cynic. Who talks like that about life?'

She paused as Rishi fell silent.

'What about Bua and Fufaji? These things lie scattered around even when they come to stay? Or do you call a professional cleaner then?'

Rishi let out a deep breath. Mira didn't know how to interpret that.

Long telephonic conversations with the coordinators of IAD and numerous visits to the bank had gone into his admissions. The coordinators had put him through to senior officials and professors, who had guided him thoroughly, much before the admissions had taken place. The bank approved an educational loan, infuriating his parents further. Not wanting to revisit that part of his life, Rishi just said, 'They don't come here. They believe that after I've wasted a few years trying to make a career out of art, I'll go back to them crying. They are waiting to receive me back at home, frustrated and defeated, ready to be enrolled on, as you said the other day, something "academic"!'

This time Mira kept quiet.

6.

Late in the night, the cousins lay looking out of their bedside window. They stared at the moon shining bright in the sky. After a few days of incessant rains, the clouds had taken a break. For a change, the slum was quiet. Old lanterns blackened with soot illuminated the windows as much as they could. The dirty passage, usually populated and buzzing, looked haunted. Coconut trees swayed in the background. Buildings stood like dark sentinels on the horizon, and grey clouds floated above them in silence.

Mumbai didn't witness too many such evenings. That day there had been a short circuit somewhere. The street lights were off; fans and air-conditioners weren't working; the Wi-Fi was off. Many residents had climbed up to the terrace, perhaps for the first time, and were pleasantly surprised to see the bright full moon.

'This girl is still so innocent,' Rishi thought as he quietly reached for the camera. There was not much difference between the little girl in Shimla and the young woman now. She was diffident and vulnerable, with a face that God must have crafted with care. The large eyes, long nose and full lips made her look stunning even on a tired evening when she was just waiting to retire. Mira was now propped up on the pillow, her chin cushioned into its soft recesses. The moonlight was falling obliquely on her face. Her hair, unkempt, had fallen across her face and back; sleepy eyes looked dreamily into the distance. It was a beautiful frame. Rishi's eyes narrowed. He waited for the perfect moment, aimed his camera and pressed the shutter.

She protested. 'What are you doing?'

Rishi looked at the shot. Marvellous. The shadows cast by the window grill were engaged in an exotic interplay with the moonlight that fell like silver on her face. In that moment suspended in time, her drowsy eyes gazed at some uncertain, distant, purposeless haven. He looked at Mira. She was frowning at him, her sleep gone.

'Show!' she commanded.

Rishi burst out laughing. 'How typical of you, Mira. Weren't you dying to crash just two seconds back? One click and you ditch the bed.'

Without a word, Mira took the camera from his hands. She smiled at what she saw on the screen. She turned on her side, pulled her knees up to her chest and looked at her cousin.

'You are good at it, you know.'

Rishi's eyes shone with mischief. 'Yeah. Otherwise when on earth have you ever looked that pretty?'

Mira raised her hand to slap him. Rishi moved away just in time, and Mira's hand came down on the bed. She rolled her eyes.

'By the way, you kicked me in your sleep last night,' she said.

'I did? Really?' Rishi sat up in bed.

'What are you doing?' Mira pulled herself up too. 'Where are you going?'

Rishi's smiled impishly again as he picked up his pillow.

'Not that you don't deserve to be kicked, Browny, but not when I am sleeping. I'd rather have the pleasure of kicking you when I am wide awake.'

'Rishi!' Mira cried out, shocked. 'I didn't mean that. Please don't.'

But the brother was already spreading a bed sheet on the ground. She sprang out of bed and tried to pull him up by the elbow, embarrassed.

Rishi looked at her and smiled. 'Browny, don't look so sorry. It's fine. You might get hurt in your sleep. I do have a mean kick.' He grinned.

Mira looked a little settled with that logic. 'Fine, then, but we take turns to sleep on the floor.'

'Done deal.'

A few minutes of silence passed before Mira spoke from the bed. 'You asleep?'

Rishi opened his eyes to find her looking outside the window again. 'Not as long as you are awake!' he sighed.

She ignored the sarcasm. 'Remember those nights in Shimla?'

They both fell silent. The snow-clad hills, the black sal trees, the faint light filtering through the windows of the small huts thrown in between, the trudge of the children walking to school, Mall Road, the bells of the Sunday church, the siren of the motor factory at 7.30 in the morning, the smell of soft, warm bread and the songs Shiraz sang as he tended the marigolds—all rushed into that small one-room apartment in Mumbai. The moon in Shimla once fell on nature like molten pearl—now it felt like demolished memoirs from the past.

The cousins didn't speak. One word from either would have

crushed those images and thrown them back into the bigoted present. When Rishi opened his mouth, it was to gently hum a song. Mira listened till he finished.

'You still remember it.' Her eyes looked at the rolling clouds outside.

'Shiraz would sing this so often.' Rishi returned a smile that was sadder than tears. 'He was a folk singer. He was called to local parties and fairs to perform. Coarse voice, rugged chords. The language of the mountains. His special affection for orange marigolds in the garden—his life was interlinked with those flower beds. His desperate savings to buy a green sari for his wife and silver foot ornaments for his daughter by Eid… All these recycled as the lyrics of his songs.' Rishi looked at Mira. 'How does he look these days? I don't think he can ever grow old!'

The thousand shackles that tugged at the sister's heart didn't reach Rishi. Nature had come to a standstill, the breeze outside paused by some cruel wizard. Her voice had caught in her throat but she managed to whisper, 'Your secret love story with Sunny. He bribed you with extra pieces of chicken before dinner and asked you to have them in front of Saundarya Ma. You would run straight into her lap with those chicken pieces. She would shriek in horror, shouting and cursing, and then go for a bath even on the coldest winter night!'

Both were laughing now. Despite Rishi's antics, Saundarya Ma had never complained to the Major or to his mother. She would only hunt Sunny out and give him an earful for spoiling the boy. Sunny would protest, feign ignorance, but every time he would feel proud of his partner in crime, going back to bribe him some more with culinary delights.

'Such a nitwit, that Sunny,' Rishi said, laughing. 'And what a rascal I was.'

'Yes! And you chased the butterflies out of the garden too!'

'I didn't chase them out, dumb,' Rishi protested. 'I flew with them. I romanced them. Beautiful green, blue and purple ones. They looked like fairies. They danced with me and ran away every time they spotted you invading our privacy.'

'Really? They often sat on my palms and shoulders and head. I didn't see them doing that with you.' Mira tried to dismiss his boastful romance.

'True. We agreed to keep it platonic.'

Mira threw her pillow at him; Rishi threw it back.

'Major still smokes the pipe?' he asked. 'Hey, ask him to try something new. Pipes and cigars are so clichéd with the military and the detectives. They desperately need a rebranding. Sometime I will fill weed into his pipe and he'd know life is more colourful than his monosyllabic disapprovals.'

Mira sat up in bed. The moon had shifted; it no longer shone on her face. But even in the dark, the tension in her posture was apparent. Rishi looked up at her dark silhouette. 'You look scary, Browny, like a ghost who might just spring on me,' he teased.

No response.

Rishi rolled his eyes. 'I don't smoke, Browny. But I know what happens because some of my friends do. Now sleep.'

Quietly, Mira fell back in bed. Rishi had covered his eyes with his hand again. She kept wondering why her brother needed such 'friends' and why he couldn't find better company. But in the last few days, she had learnt that not everything could be put across bluntly to Rishi. Childhood had been so much simpler. She could just walk up to him and bare her heart. Nothing that came from her could ever hurt him back then. Those days he only wanted her company. Today, he also expected support. She thought she was the only loner in the family. But increasingly it felt like Rishi was lonely too! Just of a different kind.

She was vaguely aware of the sound of the table clock ticking away to vast nothingness. Time, which had transformed a little mischievous boy into a handsome young man. Time that brought them close once again, but had changed the brother inside out and left to her the task of rediscovering him all over again. Would time also bring their parents together and help them bury their differences? Rishi had again started humming softly. The tune and words were known to her. The songs of Shiraz…

'Problem No. 3,281,' she thought. 'The interests of a brother or the sentiments of an artist?'

Random thoughts melted into sleep.

The watchman knocked on their door at 7 a.m. the next day, as torrential rains lashed the city again. Rishi was already up, sipping his morning tea.

'No maid today. She's got a bad stomach,' the guard informed him. The maid happened to be the watchman's wife.

'What if it rains tomorrow as well?' Rishi asked, but received no more than just a show of masala-stained teeth in response. He bent to pick up the newspaper and the packet of milk the vendors had left outside their door. Just as he closed the door, he heard the watchman telling the neighbour, 'No maid today. She's got fever.'

Waking up Mira felt more worthwhile than debating the status of changing morality in India. He picked up a paper bag lying on the floor, blew into it and burst it loudly next to her ear. Mira sprang up in bed with a cry. The crows and pigeons perched on the cornice fluttered away, alarmed. Mira cursed Rishi. After the initial arguments on how the morning should be spent, they decided to have breakfast outside. A quick bath and they were off.

As they rode towards IIT Bombay through the wet roads, Mira enjoyed the cool breeze playing with her hair. She nudged Rishi from behind. 'Hey, teach me to ride a bike. I rode a Scooty in Saharanpur, but a bike would be so much more fun.'

Rishi replied curtly, 'No.'

'Why?' she asked.

'Two reasons,' Rishi said from the front. 'You don't have the image of a biker. You will end up scandalizing my Kohli.'

Irritated at the mention of the cricketer again, Mira asked, 'And what's the second reason?'

'Not everyone can manage Kohli. It's either Dhoni or me!' He chuckled impishly.

They stopped at the canteen of IIT Bombay and ordered breakfast.

'Now listen to the plan,' Rishi said, munching on a huge piece of oil-stained paratha. 'Once your classes are over, hop on to a rickshaw and get yourself to IAD. I will show you around our campus and then head for dinner. Once we are back, you clean the room and I prepare the food for tomorrow. Deal?'

Mira's eyes widened. 'You can cook?'

Rishi brought his face close to hers and narrowed his eyes. 'One spoon down, you will lust for more!'

Mira kicked him hard on his foot. He made a show of pain, but laughed. He dropped her to the main building in front of the stairs. As she walked away, Kohli roared, turned in style and disappeared into a cloud of dust.

Mira walked to the door of her classroom, when there was a pat on her back. Surprised, she turned to find a slim, pretty girl smiling back at her. She assumed it was a classmate.

'Hi,' Mira smiled.

'Boyfriend?' the girl asked.

Shocked, Mira tried to understand where the question was coming from. The girl frowned.

'The guy who just dropped you,' she explained, her tone slightly harsh now.

'Cousin.' Mira tried to smile but was still stunned at the sudden intrusion, and at this girl, who was quite dominating and subtly rude.

The girl, who introduced herself as Kriti, however, made no attempt to address the air of confusion between them. She remained glued to Mira like a long-lost friend. She took the seat beside her in the classroom as they waited for their first lecture on Digital Message Transmission. Soon the professor entered and the class stood up. From behind a few taller heads and broader physiques, Mira tried to catch a glimpse of the professor. She froze. Quietly she sat down, trying her best to hide herself in the not-so-dense crowd.

He found her anyway. He seemed to make a mental note of all the faces, memorizing their names while going through the attendance sheet. The deep eyes lingered on her for a few seconds as the baritone called out her name, and moved on.

Mira tried to concentrate on the lecture, but ended up looking at his intense eyes throughout; they seemed to sparkle with intelligence from behind the golden spectacles. The blue shirt was perfectly tucked inside his beige trousers, the watch on his wrist shone every time he raised his hand to write something on the board, his command on her favourite subject was absolute, his perfect articulation and unusual accent all etched some fascinating irregular impressions in her mind. Before leaving, the professor gave the class a brief stare, as if to gauge whether they had grasped things correctly, and then in long, brisk steps, walked out.

Mira turned to her right and caught Kriti looking at her. She had been a pain all through the class, passing her chits and signalling her to respond. Mira had ignored her. Now that the class was over, there wasn't much she could do to avoid this girl who sat blocking her path, smiling weirdly.

'Where are you from?' she asked. 'You certainly didn't come to IIT Bombay for your M.Tech.'

'Shimla. Dad is posted in Saharanpur.' Mira was curt. She felt uncomfortable with Kriti.

'Small-town girl, eh! I don't blame you. Everyone reacts like that to him.'

'Whom?' Mira put her books inside her bag without looking at her. But Kriti gave no sign that she had taken the hint. She just sat there, watching Mira trying to politely avoid her.

'Professor Shayan Chatterjee, who else?' She gave Mira a smile again and rested her head on the desk behind. 'You couldn't take your eyes off him.'

Mira was turning red with anger. What does this girl think

of herself? Why was this exchange of words necessary? Why should she justify herself to a complete stranger? Why was she even talking to her?

'I was attending a lecture. We small-town girls come to big cities to study and make a career. We don't have time to waste on purposeless banter,' she blurted out. But her helplessness, more than disgust, was evident from her tone. This time Kriti stood up to make way for her. 'Hey, we, too, made careers all through B.Tech, just like you did in the last ninety minutes.' She laughed and left, leaving Mira embarrassed.

Was it really so obvious or had the girl just taken a chance? Mira left her seat and walked to the last corner bench of the room. There were no windows near it, so no one would see what she was looking at on her laptop. She started it up and typed in the website of IIT Bombay. Before joining here she had scrolled through the list of professors without really paying much attention. This time she browsed the list and located Professor Shayan Chatterjee. There he was. The photograph on the website seemed to have passed through a coal mine before it was uploaded. It was forty shades darker than his real complexion, and his eyes seemed to be popping out of his face, probably because of the flash. She giggled. No one would ever know from this image that it belonged to one of the smartest men she had ever seen. She gorged on the qualifications—Ph.D. from Kansas State University, then four years spent working in its research centres; back to Mumbai some seven years ago; consulting with endless institutions since then, one of them being IIT Bombay.

'So he's not a full-timer here,' Mira thought. 'He comes for specific days and allotted hours.' She was about to shut down when the sound of a whistle startled her. She looked up to find Kriti standing at the door of the classroom. Mira immediately grew conscious, scared that her little secret would be out in front of this loudmouth. In slow steps, Kriti entered the room, still whistling, but made no attempt to come near Mira.

'Tell me, babes, that the site open on your laptop right now is not the list of professors at IIT Bombay. You say no, I believe, I leave.' She stood with her hands across her chest.

Mira wanted to tell her to leave her alone. But as much as she wanted to, she couldn't convince herself that she would be able to pull it off. She ended up laughing and covered her face. Kriti walked towards her. 'We all did that, you know, believing that it was our darkest secret, that no one would ever know that we had looked him up. But the fact is, every girl and every guy in IIT Bombay knows that the first test they flunk on this campus has nothing to do with academics.'

Kriti sat beside her and looked at the photograph on the screen. 'Just look at him. Looks like a criminal from Tihar Jail.' Both of them laughed. Kriti looked at Mira again and extended her hand. 'If you are done with your inhibitions, then we might as well be friends.' Mira returned the gesture, somewhat hesitantly; they locked hands. Kriti tapped her cheek where usually a dimple appeared when she smiled. 'Smile back,' she said. 'I am not after your life. But your bro is hot. His jawline is to die for, you know? Of course you don't. Sisters don't look at their brothers' jawlines.'

She walked away.

7.

Rishi checked his watch. It was 5.30 in the evening. He was just about to dial Mira's number from his mobile when a message from her read, 'On my way.' He messaged back his floor and class and went back to work.

Jehangir Art Gallery was hosting an exhibition in association with a leading advertising agency called Buffers Inc. Buffers was the dream company for anyone who wanted to be anything in advertising and motion graphics. A hundred students across India were shortlisted to share a platform for Applied Arts. Along with the prices for the exhibits, job offers and internships would be negotiated on the floor. Selection procedures would be stringent and the competition tough. He picked up the 35×25-inch canvas lying half done and set it up erect. He looked at Poncho. He was catching up on his daily nap. Slowly Rishi walked up to him. Poncho sat with his back against the wall, head tucked between his knees, and snored softly. Rishi kicked him; Poncho fell on his side.

'What the...!' He started, and looked up to find Rishi frowning down at him. He relaxed but still protested. 'Why are you torturing me after class?' He rubbed his eyes.

'I need help.' Rishi pointed to the canvas.

Not impressed, Poncho yawned. 'My creativity is not at its peak when I am sleepy.'

Rishi almost raised his leg to plant another kick, when Poncho hauled himself up and staggered towards the canvas.

'Why do you have to sleep so much?' Rishi asked. 'I don't know of any damsel who would be keeping you awake at night. So what do you do?'

'These days dad needs me to work with him on an order. Two huge line-ups are pending. Client wants a boutique job. He's specially designing some for an upcoming hotel, and the other for an NRI club to be hosted by the Hindujas. The hotelier wants uneven tiling.' He rubbed his eyes. 'Hey, why don't you come to the factory sometime? Tell me what you think. Dad was asking for you the other day.'

Rishi smiled. That was another advantage of teaming up with Poncho. 'Dad was asking for you' meant there was work.

His father's tile business worked for big names in the industry. From builders and interior designers to art house auctioneers, he was seen with the who's who of the world. Poncho was rather naïve compared to his father's association with the world of glamour. His dependence on Rishi, hence, was more than welcome. This was his investment. He pampered Poncho's reliance on him and ensured it remained like that.

'I'll come. Let's do sensuous mermaids for the men's restroom?' Rishi said without looking at him. He could sense Poncho's eyes widening. 'You are my bro! My real bro from another mother!' Poncho jumped up and hugged him. Rishi was pushed back two steps by the sudden force of Poncho's bulk but managed to balance himself. When this overflow of emotion continued, Rishi shoved him away. 'Buzz off, you cheap, smelly gimmick! All that I get at the end of a hard day's work is a hug from this pot-bellied creature.' He winked. 'Go get me a ravishing mermaid instead.'

Poncho loosened his hold, but straightened up as his eyes fell on something to their left.

'There's one standing at the door,' he said as softly as he could.

Rishi turned to look. Mira stood hesitating at the entrance, waiting to be asked inside. For a few seconds he was torn between an overwhelming urge to punch Poncho in the face for ogling at his sister and the need to address the girl who wouldn't enter unless invited. He ignored his friend and turned to Mira. 'What are you standing there for, Brow...er...Mira? Come on in.'

He introduced her to Poncho, who shook hands a bit too generously and a bit too long, a big smile on his face. He offered to get tea or coffee from the canteen. Rishi ignored his chivalrous advances and pointed at the canvas. 'Prepare the base.'

Poncho grimaced. 'To hell with you, bugger.' Quietly, he started arranging the paints and the brushes.

In less than an hour, Rishi's bike was racing through the Western Express Highway. Mira asked about the shops and lanes they crossed and Rishi showed her the landmarks in between—the stretch of sea as they reached Bandra, Lilavati Hospital, the Linking Road markets, the graffiti on Chapel Road and Mount Mary's Church.

When they reached Bandstand, a loud 'Stop!' from Mira made him skid to an abrupt halt. She jumped down and looked dreamily at the palace-like building in front. Without looking in the direction of his sister's gaze, Rishi groaned.

'No, Browny, stop behaving like a lunatic. People are watching.'

Mira didn't speak, neither did she move. Rishi couldn't help chuckling as he looked at his cousin, rooted to the spot, mouth slightly open in awe, eyes still fixed on the gate. Then a little loudly, he repeated, 'Browny, let's go.'

This time she turned. 'Stop calling me that. You almost introduced me to Vidit as Browny.'

Who? Rishi almost asked. Then he remembered. Poncho's formal name was Vidit! Ambitious, high-society parents wanted him to be Vidit; the duffer pulled their expectations down to ashes and became Poncho. He grinned, but his smile disappeared with the next sentence Mira uttered softly in his ear.

'Hey, can we walk up to the guards and ask if he's inside?'

Rishi pulled Mira towards the bike and gestured her to sit. 'No. Get back on the bike.'

She didn't seem to be affected at all. She didn't even look at him. She just strained to get a better look beyond the gates. 'Look at how they are posing,' she whispered and giggled. 'The tall guy just yelled at the fat boy because he clicked a picture of him without the nameplate.'

This time Rishi turned to look at Shah Rukh Khan's residence, Mannat. People indeed left their brains at home when they came here. Once, some college students had gathered at the same stretch, dancing to popular songs of SRK quite late in the night. They had no clue whether the superstar was watching them. They danced to his songs wildly till a watchman showered them with abuses. They disappeared. Next day a YouTube video of their performance went viral on the Internet. It even captured the watchman shouting at them. In the next two days, someone made a rap out of the watchman's words and that, too, went viral!

'Should we go?' he asked again, looking away from the palace.

'Yes. Let's go and ask.' Mira ran forward.

Rishi jumped down from the bike and ran after her to catch her by the arm, dragging her backwards, both of them laughing hysterically. Mira wiped her eyes. Rishi quietly sat on his bike and started it without another word. This time Mira sensed trouble; she quickly hopped on behind him, still giggling.

'You are a Shah Rukh Khan fan?' he asked as they rode.

'Who isn't?' she sighed dreamily.

'Too generic. If you are a Shah Rukh Khan fan, you become part of the masses. Predictable and easy.'

Mira frowned. 'Don't even try! Else I'll get you thrashed by the SRK fans here.'

They stopped at the Café Coffee Day on Carter Road. After ordering coffee and snacks, Mira broached the topic she had been dying to discuss.

'There's this classmate I have, she wants to meet you.' She expected to surprise her cousin.

'The fair girl in the blue tee and cargoes?' he asked, munching on a sandwich.

'How do you know?' Mira was shocked.

'She was ogling at us from the corner of the stairs.'

Her coffee grew cold on the table. 'Is that all? No excitement?'

Rishi smiled. If only she knew the crowd in his campus! He watched Mira take a sip of coffee and grimace. It had turned tasteless. Trying not to disappoint her further, he asked, 'What did she tell you?'

'Nothing. Initially I felt she was encroaching too much. But later I realized she's nice. We're friends now.' She tried to smile. Her sudden discomfort didn't elude Rishi, but he chose not to ask. 'She has done her B.Tech from IIT Mumbai. So she knows this place better. Good that we became friends. She'll be able to guide me around stuff.' Mira was almost talking to herself.

'What do you suggest? Should I meet her?' Rishi looked at her, cuffing his mouth with his fist.

'I don't know, but that's what she expects you to do!'

He stared. 'So should I follow her expectations or mine?'

The question unsettled Mira. What did it even mean? Did she even know what her own expectations were from herself? When had anyone expected anything from her, other than that she would keep letting the wheel of life turn, moving forward, irrespective of the destination?

Were men in big cities usually so passive? Of course not. But then, wasn't Professor Chatterjee also equally indifferent? Kriti had told her that he knew the girls on the campus would do anything to get his attention but he didn't ever stop to say a word that went beyond academics. It was difficult for her, though, to comprehend that her little brother, too, received that kind of attention from women. Rishi was mischievous, focused and flamboyant. But 'women's dream' material?

But then, why not? She debated in her mind. He was handsome, smart, ambitious and funny. That must be an attractive combination.

Problem No. 3,292: Rishi and women.

I'll ask Kriti tomorrow what's so appealing about this duffer, she made a mental note. Aloud, she charged Rishi. 'You have a problem with girls?'

Rishi looked at her. 'No, I enjoy them.' A wicked smile

crept across his face again. 'But I prefer a Virat Kohli over a Shah Rukh. You know what I mean? Substance over swag. That Kriti is eye candy, she'd be a pressure on the arm.'

'Did anyone tell you that you are the biggest moron on earth?' Mira tried to shut him off, but in vain.

'Your Kriti is looking for a fling. That's nice to know, but expensive to handle.' He yawned. Mira sat there, hopelessly taken aback. She didn't like the word 'fling'. He waited for her to voice her disapproval. She didn't, but seemed upset, her innocence shaken.

'Wait till the girl asks for a portrait or a painting. She may even hope I'll do a photoshoot of her.' He tried to keep the conversation going.

Unable to comprehend where this was coming from, Mira frowned. 'Why would she?'

'Two-third of the world believes that the only way to motivate an artist is to express interest in his work by asking for freebies.' Rishi turned to signal to the waiter hovering around their table for the bill.

Poor, innocent Browny, he thought. She had never met enough people to understand how much was left unsaid in every conversation. God knows what she was doing in those four years of B.Tech. Her simplicity worried Rishi. His sister had led a cushioned life for a very long time. He could sense in her an urge, a desperation, to break free and explore. It was so subtly embedded in her subconscious that even she didn't quite recognize it. Mira had been raised too conservatively, sheltered by guardians who treated her like a feather. He needed to help her come into her own, albeit safely.

'You know, Browny,' Rishi bent forward, as Mira gobbled

down her pastry, 'women can inspire and women can distract. At this stage, a distraction would be too costly for me.' He smiled and settled back in his seat.

8.

Inspire! Such a beautiful word.

Mira had always loved Rishi's clarity of thought, be it in life, in career or in his ambition. There were days when he needed 'space'—a word she had heard much but knew nothing about. He stayed withdrawn, glued to his laptop or reading something. He'd forget to shave, talk less and spend a lot of time at home. Thinking something was wrong, Mira had tried to talk him out of the reserve, but he had just returned monosyllabic answers. 'Just working on something, Browny,' was all he would say. It felt horrible wondering what she must have done to irk him into hopeless withdrawal.

After a few days of that torture last time, one evening she was leaving her campus, when the tea stall near the Y.P. gate caught her eye. It was located just below a construction site. Students flocked there for tea, usually on somebody else's money or on credit. The stall was strangely empty that evening. The only customer it had was her cousin. Slightly unsure, she walked towards him in slow steps.

'I called you, you didn't pick up, so I thought you must be in class. I left a text,' he said, sipping the tea the old man at the shop had made, probably from the same tea leaves he had used for his first customer in the morning. He held out a cup towards her too, and she sat down beside him.

'From now on, Browny, I will wait for you here at Kunj Bihariji's stall. He is a good man.'

The old man smiled ear to ear, pleased with the importance he was suddenly receiving. Kunj Bihari! He liked the name—it was fancy. Mira didn't care whether he was Kunj Bihari or Kumudini. What mattered was that her cousin was behaving normally again.

Rishi turned towards the old man. 'Kunj Bihari Sahab, one more, please.'

'I didn't see your text,' Mira ventured. 'My phone was inside the bag.'

A big envelope lay beside Rishi. He moved it towards her. She opened it and took out a large photograph. Her photograph! Awestruck, she placed it on the grass to take a full look. Kunj Bihari raised himself on his toes to take a better look from behind the counter, while his expert hands arranged for the repeat order.

This was the one that Rishi had clicked the night of the full moon, but it had a completely different character now. The print in front of her showed an old wall with cracks and spiderwebs. The window and the grills in it were rusted. An eighteenth-century clock hung from the top, its hands hidden in the dark, just its frame silhouetted against the cracked wall. From one such crack, a creeper had crawled out, its roots and leaves threatening to take over. The moonlight, though, still fell on her face, as it had in the original shot, and she was sitting in the same posture as she had that night, dressed in silk.

'Unbelievable,' she breathed, unable to take her eyes off the photograph. Kunj Bihari didn't understand much, though, and went back to boiling the already-boiled tea. Why should a pretty girl be thrown amid ruins and broken walls? He nodded but knew better than to open his mouth.

Rishi put the photograph back in the envelope. 'Photoshop and graphics,' he smiled. 'It's magic. The art of transformation, treading somewhere between imagination and reality. You know, it allows the brain to recreate reality. Because sometimes, what you see isn't really how you see it.'

The photograph was going up as an exhibit at a show, he told her.

❊

Two days later, Rishi's words still echoing in her mind, Mira entered the branch of Canara Bank inside the campus. It had been raining since morning; the floor of the bank was splotched with muddy shoe prints. She shivered a little as the cold air from the air conditioner hit her damp clothes. She sneezed.

She needed to fill up a slip and reached inside her bag for a pen. It wasn't there. Helplessly, she looked around for someone she could borrow one from. There was no one she knew. Left with no choice, she approached the last figure in the teller queue. He turned and slipped his pen into her hand. Mira froze. The man now looking down at her, his eyes as nonchalant as the teller's, was Professor Shayan Chatterjee. For a few seconds Mira didn't know how to react. Confused and tense, she stammered. 'Sir…no…that…I really had my own pen in my bag…but my friend…classmate…she didn't return. No, Sir, I really didn't mean to bother you…Didn't know it was you. From behind you looked different. I mean I didn't see who you were before I asked. Sorry, Sir. No pen. I'll manage.

Don't bother, Sir…it's okay!' She held the pen out for him to take it back.

The man's face registered no reaction. As she fumbled for words, his ice-cold eyes sat motionless on her bewildered ones. He looked at the pen she was holding out, then back at her, and quietly took it away. He waited, watching her.

For a few seconds, Mira couldn't believe that he had actually taken the pen away. She needed it. He knew, but didn't insist on her having it. She looked at her empty hand. His eyes, still fixed on her, only made her fidgety. Again, she frantically searched her bag. Of course she didn't have a pen. She looked at him again, as he watched her indifferently. Suddenly in panic, she looked around for someone else to approach, so she could show a pen to Professor Chatterjee and prompt him to look elsewhere. She almost ran to seek help from a stranger, when a hand came forward again, holding the same damn pen out to her. Unsteadily, she took it this time. There was a kind of disdain in his eyes now. He finally turned back to the queue, much to Mira's relief.

It took her a while to recollect why she needed the pen in the first place. Quickly, she scribbled her details on the slip. Too many blank spaces to be filled required her to refer to her bank statements. Next time she would memorize these to avoid the fuss, she promised herself. Once done, she turned to return the pen. This time she had to talk smartly, not behave like a lunatic. But there was no Professor Chatterjee in the teller line. He wasn't anywhere in the bank either. She tried to ask a few people around.

'A tall and handsome…no, not handsome…nice, yes…nice, helpful man standing here in a white shirt?' They looked at her as if she were unhinged and had just asked for a route to the moon. The only help they offered was a shake of the head confirming they saw or remembered no such man—his whereabouts weren't their concern.

Mira ran back to the campus, ignoring the torrential rains. By the time she reached, she was drenched. The research assistant told her the professor had left for the day. Mira looked down at the pen—a beautiful, expensive silver Sheaffer. He had left it with her so casually. She wrapped the pen in a piece of paper and a handkerchief, and tucked it into the safest corner of her bag. Neither the rains nor Kriti must find it.

All through the evening she had been trying to concentrate on the books open before her. The mid-semester exams were lined up next week and she needed to gear up. She had sneezed some fourteen times and even the handkerchief wanted to revolt. At frequent intervals she touched her bag to ensure that the pen was still there. Every time she tried to concentrate, the man in the white shirt stared at her. While passing her the pen, their hands had touched. She quivered at the adventure of that fleeting second. She wished there had been more to the unexpected meeting. He could have offered to drop her home or even just waited for her to return the pen. But the way she had turned nervous, anyone would run away. If only he would smile a little. She had never seen this Chatterjee smiling. If only he would tell her something...anything! From the latest controversy where a starlet got trolled for suggesting that Shah Rukh Khan's shirt at a social do was a bad match for his blazer, to the rising militant warfare in Europe, to the status of the India-Pakistan friendship, there were so many things people talked about all the time. Couldn't he find even one topic to broach?

Mira hit herself with the book and tried to concentrate again. Tough luck. She just ended up looking out of the window, lost in thoughts of his almond skin. She was jolted back to reality when the door of the room clicked open. Rishi had entered, drained after a tough day. He went for a shower. By the time Mira had heated the food and brought him a plate, he was lying in bed, fast asleep. She covered his food and went back to her textbooks. This time no more daydreaming. One of the assignments scheduled for the week ahead was for Professor Chatterjee's subject—she couldn't afford to flunk that. Rather, she'd have to score the highest in that paper.

Rishi woke up around 7.30 p.m. and immediately switched on the small television set kept in the corner of the room. Mira protested. She was deep into her studies by then.

'It's an India-Australia match, Browny,' Rishi cried. But to make things easier for Mira, he watched the match on mute. The team had just won the toss and chosen to bowl first. Other than occasional bouts of excitement, he tried not to make it too distracting for his sister.

Mira studied for a few more hours and didn't realize when she slept off, her textbook held close to her chest. She had been dreaming of bright romantic eyes looking at her from behind a pair of golden spectacles when the brother threw his arms up and shouted, 'Marry me, Virat Kohli!'

Mira sat up straight in bed. It took her some time to fathom that the Delhi boy had sculpted a power-packed innings, chasing an impossible target set by the Aussies. He had once again dismissed their bowlers like Rajnikanth disposed of villains. His bat had sent the ball beyond the gallery as though they were kisses to his girlfriend. The lad had won the match for India by six wickets. There were fireworks outside. On the screen of the mute television set, the audience had broken into energetic jigs. Uncles danced unmindful of the heart attack they might be inviting. Rishi joined them from this side of the screen—unbeatable bhangra without music. Mira's irritation vanished under this euphoric madness. Neither could she say no when her brother suggested they go out for a coffee celebration at night.

He zoomed his Kohli ahead to reach the coffee shop owned by the widowed Mrs Maheshwari on her open terrace. After her husband's death, the neighbours had advised and helped the lonely, middle-aged woman set up this café. Rishi had done up some of the interiors, for which Mrs Maheshwari was ever grateful. It opened around 7 in the evening and stayed open all through the night. Countless people came here to keep it buzzing. If all chairs were occupied, people sat on the floor. A fleet of stairs outside the bungalow went straight up to the terrace. A crowd of cricket fans had already gathered there. Youngsters and the elderly alike were dancing and hugging each other. Even the two police officers, who had probably come to check the volume of music, were standing on a corner of the street—smoking, smiling, greeting everyone with 'Jai Bharat, Jai Maharashtra!'. To one of them, Rishi shouted, 'Mama, coming upstairs to dance?'

He showed the stick in his hand. 'Bhanja, coming with us for a treat?'

They both laughed as Rishi ran upstairs, holding Mira by the hand.

Rishi could see Mira was enjoying every bit of this new life in Mumbai. That's what Mumbai does. It connects people and yet stays aloof. The neighbours here may not come to you asking for a spoonful of sugar, but they come together to celebrate or to mourn. Interference is an offence here, togetherness meaningful. Never had she attended this kind of a late-night, open-air party. Rishi introduced her to a few more people. Young boys and girls showered her with attention, asking her all sorts of questions.

'M.Tech? IIT? She seems to be the studious type, man,' one of them said, her large eyes inspecting Mira.

'Yes, if my mother knows, she will call me a loser again,' quipped another.

One girl placed her hand on Mira's shoulder. 'See, if any of those ladies standing to your right ask you anything, please say you are from another planet.' She chuckled.

'And when you get a job, please contribute a percentage of your earnings to the Powai Educated Beggars' Association, which is currently being manned by all of us.'

They laughed and raised their hands in high fives. Rishi left his sister alone with her new friends and mingled around in the crowd with a huge latte. On and off, he carried a tray of coffee cups and snacks to the elders, with a few more joining him to help at this rush hour. From a distance, he watched Mira. She had been so stiff when she had come to Mumbai, but her walls were coming down fast. She chatted for a couple of minutes with the others before she made her way back to Rishi.

'Bonfires. Sunny lit bonfires in Shimla when India won a match. He rolled out a special spread for such evenings,' Rishi reminisced. 'It was Major Sahab who taught me the rules of cricket. He introduced me to various kinds of shots.'

Mira smiled. Her father was better known as Major Sahab than any other name or relationship that could define him. Rishi's father called him that, and soon, from the staff of the house to the neighbours, everyone called him by that name.

'He, too, danced and ordered his special drink every time India won. Every time I missed a catch while playing with him, he would cough out a curse at me.' They both laughed as Rishi imitated his uncle.

'We must do something, Browny,' he suddenly said, turning to Mira.

'What can we do, Rishi? Sharat Uncle tried so much. But neither Bua, nor Dad was willing to listen.'

'It's not about just my dad trying,' Rishi said thoughtfully. 'He can't control my mom anyway. But maybe we can. We have to.'

'How?' Mira asked sadly.

For a moment her brother looked at her. Then his eyes brightened.

'Let's make them meet. Somehow. I am sure mom will cry if she meets you guys after so many years. And Major Sahab won't be able to ignore us and leave.' He hit his palm with his fist. Mira evaluated the plan.

'Yes, that's the way we should do it. Let's just bring them together!' Rishi said again. 'Just that we will have to play it safe. If they understand what we are up to, they'll come down on us.'

This needed thorough thinking. They left the café with this one new thought in their brains, along with the academic and professional targets both were racing to fulfil.

9.

The next evening, Rishi reached Kunj Bihari's stall early. There was a lot of work pending at the lab, but he needed a break. Leaving Poncho with strict instructions, he reached the tea stall and made himself comfortable on the bench. The monsoons were off and the heat was back.

'How's life, Kunj Bihariji?' He wiped the sweat off his brow and received a resigned nod in return.

'Too much heat, Sir. People don't want tea in this heat; they are going for fruit juice from that corrupt vendor across the road. That bugger fills up only half the glass with juice and tops it up with dirty ice. I have lost so many customers to him lately.'

Rishi smiled. 'Don't worry. I will make up for some of it. Get me a big glass, please.'

The old man grinned and lit up his burner.

Rishi took out his sketchbook and charcoal pencil. The view from here was exotic. A banyan tree stood in front of the tea stall, offering its customers some much-needed shade. The cracks on the bark of the tree, the mesh of offshoots sprouting from the trunk, the thousand perforations on its body that were home to millions of insects, the birds chirping from the sturdy branches above and the prop roots suspended from them like dreadlocks, all led to a strange, isolated calm. Even on days the tea stall was bustling with customers, the banyan tree stood sombrely apart, maintaining a strict distance from the excitement of the current generation. Thousands of passers-by over the years had carved out an unsteady path on the grass beside it, connecting the tea stall to the inroads of IIT Bombay across the open field. A few cars and bikes drove past in the distance. Kunj Bihari's radio played a Mohammad Rafi classic.

With swift strokes of his charcoal pencil, Rishi started capturing this moment in his sketchbook. His mind interpreted more than his eyes saw. Briskly, his pencil moved across the thick paper to recreate the truth before him. A tired boy sat at the foot of the banyan tree, his face buried between his knees. The prop roots formed a brown curtain around him, hiding everything he wanted to conceal from a world that had little time for him.

Rishi frequently looked up to draw visual clues from the scene in front. Little did he know that another customer had approached the stall. He was made aware of his presence only when he chose to stand blocking his view. Irritated with the intrusion, he called out roughly, 'Excuse me. Stand aside, please.' He went back to work.

The man turned. Unaccustomed to being spoken to in that tone, Professor Shayan Chatterjee walked back towards Rishi to watch him sketching fine lines, shading some of the corners with steady, rapid strokes, and diffusing a few bold contours with the tip of his finger to cast a shadow.

'Nice.' The word escaped his mouth even before he meant it to be heard.

'Thanks,' Rishi acknowledged without looking at him.

'Aren't the mid-semesters around the corner? Why are you

wasting time like this?' This made Rishi stop. Before he could say anything, the man asked him another question. 'Which department?'

A little amused now, Rishi looked at the professor. Though young and lean, the man looked hopelessly sad. A soft smile formed on his face, and he went back to his sketchbook.

Shayan Chatterjee was offended. The smile was worse than sarcasm. He frowned.

'Are you a professor or a ragging-starved senior?' Rishi asked innocently. 'Sorry, since I don't attend classes, I am not aware of who's who here.'

Cold eyes held him for a moment before showing a flicker of anger. But Rishi was enjoying himself now. He had found something other than the scene in front to light up a mundane summer evening.

'You look confused. Happens when you are meddling in other people's lives. Okay, now try to remember who you are. We'll talk when you do.' Rishi picked up his pencil again and went back to work.

Shayan had taken on many professional battles. He had a history of nasty conflicts with the lobbies of unfair diplomats and departmental politics. But this generation was beyond his comprehension. Did this young boy just shrug off his concern as abusive intervention? These kids could make a mess of their lives and no one was supposed to utter a word? Just the other day, a boy was found outside the dean's office, hoping that the Disciplinary Action Committee would work a miracle to save him. But the DAC was not a reformer! He had to be expelled because of indiscipline, and the ones worst affected were the parents. Their dreams were shattered and their hard-earned money wasted on an irresponsible creature.

'Get up and come with me,' he demanded.

Rishi made no attempt to move. His eyes still flicked from the field to his sketchbook, his fingers moving deftly across the page. 'You are a student, then,' he said simply.

'What?' The professor was growing increasingly impatient with the boy's audacity.

'Usually it's the students who give wrong answers to the questions asked.'

Shayan wanted to slap him. He took a deep breath and tightened his fist to control the anger that threatened to seize him. He wondered what he should say next to this reckless boy, who certainly didn't care about his future at IIT Bombay, but he definitely didn't want to leave without giving him a piece of his mind.

The silence made the boy look up again, his mischievous smile betraying how much he was enjoying the professor's plight. Shayan's eyes went past him, having spotted someone behind him. He turned to find out who.

Mira was walking towards them in long strides. Rishi had messaged that he had reached the campus way before time. If Kriti found him, Rishi would be mad at her. She wanted to leave at the earliest. From a distance, though, her legs threatened to give way. What was Professor Chatterjee doing there with Rishi? He seemed to be talking to him! Couldn't life just get a little simpler?

That morning Mira had reached college early. She had placed the pen inside a long, white envelope and neatly written out the professor's full name on it. She had ensured it was her best handwriting. She had entered his cabin stealthily when it was being cleaned in the morning and placed the envelope on his table. Quietly, she had gone back to class. She had expected to see him during the day or, at least, pass by him at some opportune moment. That hadn't happened.

As she approached the tea stall now, their eyes met. He looked angry. Her eyes hovered down to his shirt pocket, where he usually hung his pen. It was there. She looked back at him. He watched her doing that. Of course he wasn't going to thank her or say anything about the envelope or her handwriting!

'Good morning…afternoon…evening, Sir!' she stammered. Shayan's jawline tightened and Rishi laughed loudly. They both turned to look at him.

'What is good morning…afternoon…evening, Mira?'

'Shut up!' Mira wanted to snap, but found no voice. Petrified, she looked at the professor. He spoke to her for the first time.

'Is he your friend?'

'No, Sir. Sir, cousin. Comes to drop or pick me up sometimes. IAD…Andheri…student…Graphics. What happened, Sir?'

The thin lines creasing the professor's forehead seemed to even out. He looked at Rishi—he had now stretched his legs and sat relaxed, staring at him and still laughing. A soft smile appeared on the professor's face.

'Had I been a student here, Sir, I would be as sulky as all the nice people here.' He stood up to extend his hand. 'Rishi Bahl.'

Mira almost died. But she was equally stunned. Was the professor smiling? Really? She wanted to step in front and take a closer look at his face. Unfortunately, that wasn't possible.

Shayan stretched out his hand too. 'Dr Shayan Chatterjee.'

He paused and added, 'Sulky we are, but generous enough to allow others to sit and sketch on our campus. Not sure whether your college would allow us to perform some of our practicals there.'

'Spare us,' Rishi laughed. 'IIT guys take a lot of pride in calculating 1562.3 x 439.86 orally, their arrogance oozing out of each decimal point. We are happy being the more useless variety. Colours usually don't culminate in high-power glasses—graphs do.'

Professor Chatterjee slapped his arm gently with a file. 'Let me know if you need an updated version of your graphics tools. The bespectacled people here might just come to your rescue,' he said, before walking off in long, steady strides.

Rishi smiled from behind. 'Smart chap! Just a little temperamental.' He looked at Mira, who was still gaping at the professor. He frowned and snapped his fingers in front of her face.

'What?' She looked startled.

'That question would be more apt if I asked it. What happened to you?'

Mira narrowed her eyes at him. 'Were you just fighting with him? He's our Communications professor!'

'So?' Rishi asked. 'He's not *my* professor. And he was the one to come and start lecturing me about studying for the mid-semesters. Without any background, he just starts firing off. Funny! But what's your problem?'

'Nothing.'

Mira felt it was a bad time to talk about this. Quietly, she hopped on to the pillion seat of the bike. The bike expertly navigated the turns of the campus and sped off towards the main road. At the faculty parking, Mira spotted Professor Shayan Chatterjee's car. He was leaning against it, talking to the beauty who had joined as the new professor of Thermodynamics. The campus had immediately nicknamed her 'Sweetheart'. Regardless of their specialization, every man had stopped to talk to her. And she had spoken to everyone with a glint in her eyes, as if nothing made her happier than those little conversations. Mira frowned.

Kriti had hated her on sight. And she could see why. She saw the professor open the door of his car for the woman and walk around to get in from the other side. They disappeared from sight as Rishi turned a corner with his bike.

10.

Rishi could sense the melancholy in Mira. The sister was just flipping through the textbook, hardly studying. Her blank eyes stared in front, occasionally jerked back to the open page and then lost focus again. When this went on for quite some time, he couldn't ignore it any longer. Something was brewing.

Did she have a crush on the 'why aren't you studying' guy? Quite possible. He was quite capable of attracting his simple sister. She wasn't one to make friends easily. The hand-counted few she interacted with in Shimla eventually left the hills for big cities, pushing her more into her cocoon. Having spent most of her childhood confined to the rules of obedience, Mira had just stepped out of parental jurisdiction and bumped into a handsome, intellectual hero.

Rishi stirred the coffee he had prepared for both of them and peeped out from the kitchen. She was holding a pencil in her mouth, looking blankly at the wall. Swiftly, he carried the cups in and put one down before her. 'He is hot.' Mira looked at him, her eyes wary of what this was leading to. But she didn't utter a word. He nudged some more. 'You like him?'

'Everybody likes him.' She positioned the book to hide her face. Rishi forced the book down.

'So what next?'

'Trying to study, so that I score well in his paper. But I can't concentrate.' She threw the book down. Her brother picked it up and put it back on the bed. 'I saw him with Sweetheart today. Now don't ask who Sweetheart is. They left in the same car,' she said in a small voice, tension writ large in her big, brown eyes.

Rishi fought back laughter. The girl was still such a kid! 'Just because they went together somewhere doesn't mean they're having a scene, Browny. He might just be dropping her somewhere.' She didn't seem convinced. 'Fine, think about it. If he were to have an affair with a colleague on campus, wouldn't it spell professional doom for both of them? I don't think a man who compulsively runs around trying to discipline strangers would fall prey to politically incorrect behaviour so easily. Dating a colleague in an educational institute in India is equivalent to professional suicide.'

At this, Mira looked up. Something here made sense. But his next question drained her of confidence.

'Browny, are you ready to approach him?'

'No! Never!' she cried out. 'Are you mad?'

'Then you just want to look at the wall and waste your time thinking about how he drove off with some woman?' Rishi's eyes were fixed on her. She felt nervous. The brother tapped her head gently. 'If there's no future with him, don't let him take up so much of your time. Five years down the line, you won't like to think that some hunk in college messed up your scores.'

Mira kept quiet and smiled. 'Grandpa,' she teased.

'I have to be.' Rishi smiled back. 'I am here with a 5-year-old trapped in the body of a 24-year-old.' The sister tried to slap his arm; he moved away.

∗

Mumbai doesn't have an autumn. It has summer, monsoon and a strange stretch of time around December when it is neither hot nor cold. Mid-November is a kind of approach month to that phase. Mornings and evenings are pleasant; the day is hot and the sun furious by noon.

It was broad daylight when Rishi was walking towards the faculty rooms of IIT Bombay. Cricket commentary from an electronic device played somewhere in the background, as usual praising Virat Kohli for his up-in-the-air shots. Strange that there was a match going on and he didn't know. The faculty rooms were all huddled together in a strange, dark corner of the campus—structures built in white marble with domes on top. Creepers had attacked the buildings and gigantic cobwebs hung from doorways, making entry difficult. When Rishi pushed some of it aside, a host of butterflies in blue, green and purple fluttered away. He walked a few steps inside, and stepped right into a large bed of orange marigolds. They felt familiar. He stopped to look around. A gardener was working in a far corner of the patch. Rishi approached him from behind, and called out softly, 'Shiraz?' The man turned. Eyes as intense as they had always been, sparkled like a thousand stars. 'Rishi Baba?'

'How are you here, Shiraz?'

'I had grown tired of Shimla. You never came back. The garden was no longer the same. I left the place and travelled to so many places. And one day I got here.' He smiled again. 'Why are you here?'

The sight of Shiraz after such a long time had made Rishi forget all about Shayan Chatterjee.

'Stay here, Shiraz. I'll be back.' He walked towards the door that bore the nameplate of the professor.

Shayan Chatterjee, drowned in a pile of books, looked up as if he were waiting for Rishi. He gestured for him to enter and take a seat. Before Rishi could open his mouth, his eyes fell on a photo with Major Dhillon looking out at him from behind its glass frame. Shocked, he asked Shayan, 'How do you know him?'

The professor didn't respond. He just lifted the photograph off its hook on the wall and twirled it dangerously in his hand. Rishi frowned. The professor laughed like the devil. As he rotated the photo frame with more and more speed, it flew out of his hand and crashed loudly against the wall. Shattered glass lay on the floor.

Shaken, Rishi stood up from the chair, the earth beneath his feet threatening to slip. Shards of glass glinted on the Major's face. The sight sent a shiver down his spine. But Shayan Chatterjee just kept smiling mysteriously. And his face started to change. The face morphed into Rishi's, and he walked towards him, standing to face him as his mirror image. Rishi stumbled backwards, unsure of what any of this meant. Unable to look away from the professor's gaze, he took a few more steps backwards and...

THUD!

In the darkness around him, Rishi couldn't figure out what was happening. His elbow hurt. Something was holding on to his feet tightly—he couldn't move his legs. And then he heard Mira shouting, 'Rishi! Are you okay? What happened?'

She placed her hand on his shoulder. He looked up at his sister's dark silhouette hunched over him, her body tense. Had he been dreaming? Shiraz and the butterflies, the dome-like structures and that devil laughter of Shayan Chatterjee? For a moment he wanted to hide himself from the world and think. The dream had been stressful. He opened his eyes again. The bed sheet lay entangled around his legs. Mira got him a glass of water and he gratefully gulped it down.

'Rishi, did you just have a dream and fall off the bed?' she laughed out loud. 'Maybe you dreamt of being a ball and Virat Kohli hit you straight out of the boundary!'

'Go back to sleep, dumb.' He laughed too, and climbed into the bed.

It was 3 in the morning. Mira went back to sleep almost immediately, but Rishi couldn't. The dream wasn't just a collection of random, distorted thoughts. It had raised some questions. Why hadn't he ever gone back to the Major himself? It wasn't like everything he did had his mother's approval. He could have just gone and met him. He remembered the stories Major Sahab would tell him. The encounters he had had, the strict military training, life at the camps, the funny things that had happened when he had started training his juniors, and so many others.

'Join the Indian Army when you grow up, Rishi. It's a man's life here.' The Major's voice still roared in his ears. Almost immediately, he stopped this line of thought.

'It's good that I haven't gone to meet the Major.' Sadness gripped his heart. 'He would have asked me whether I was joining the Army. Once again, one more person in my life would have been disappointed. One more person who would tell me that I am wasting my life in Applied Arts.'

Quietly he got up and opened his laptop. He had the scanned copies of a few old photographs. He looked at the one clicked by one of the Major's friends when the man had been in his early twenties; he had just joined the National Defence Academy. This photograph was taken inside a train, as the Major sat looking outside the window. Rishi smiled as he gazed at the photograph. There was no bigger solace than drowning in work when tense or sad. Perhaps the sense of helplessness inspired an energy that brought out the best in you.

It had happened many times in the past. When he didn't have an immediate answer to life's complex dilemmas, he would immerse himself in work. While his hands busied themselves in processing complicated designs on the image, the knots in his thinking disentangled. The decision to take up Arts instead of Science after fantastic results in 10th board examinations, to enrol for Comparative Literature instead of Economics after his 12th, finally ending up in an Applied Arts course against the wishes of his family, taking the educational loan—all had been mulled over while working. Now he earned some moolah by selling his work and from the assignments forwarded by Poncho's father. The money his parents sent lay unused in the bank.

Once again, the prospect of work calmed him down, as he looked at the photograph of the Major, sitting idly inside the train. His brain roiled with creative ideas. The next few days Rishi almost locked himself in the lab, where no one other than Poncho had access to him. Soon, what stared back at him was nothing less than a wonder.

He had placed a faded photograph of himself behind his uncle, peeping over his shoulder. It seemed like he was a spirit, as his image had a kind of transparency to it. Outside the window of the train, the passing scenery was blurred. From the other side, two men looked on blankly, as if wondering if that speed could be captured or protected. The uncle remained as he was; on his own face, Rishi added wrinkles, a receding hairline and slacker jaws. The inside of the train was transformed into a collection of broken bricks carelessly cemented together. A journey where uncle and nephew were trapped in time. The Major still seemed to be the strong man from his youth; but Rishi was affected by everything that had been lost in the past few years. Within the closed compartment of the train, uncle and nephew were together. Outside the window, the indefinite infinite blur wouldn't spare either.

This work, titled *Illusion*, was Rishi's last entry for the upcoming exhibition. He was one of the eight finalists selected across India to exhibit at Jehangir Art Gallery. The participants were expecting plush offers on the floor. Professors were optimistic about *Illusion*. It was selected by media partners as the invitation image, to be up on hoardings and newspapers. Only Rishi knew that this one wasn't for sale. It was meant to be his gift to the Major. His uncle may not appreciate it, but he wanted the raw emotions in the frame to reach out to his uncle and tell him everything that Rishi couldn't.

11.

Kriti picked up one of the biggest pieces from the box of sweets Mira had opened. 'Very unfair,' she complained. 'He should have brought the sweets himself!'

Mira laughed. 'Go catch him and ask.'

Kriti made a face. 'Oh, please! Your bro is a snob. I tried to talk to him so many times. He made it very clear that he wasn't interested.'

Mira looked away. 'He's not a snob. He's practical. He treats his time like money.' *Spend it to buy fun but never give away to the undeserved.* The illustration that had gained him so many accolades was also a reflection of time—the time that belonged to both Rishi and her father, but neither could really own it.

Everyone was shocked when Rishi had declared the image was not for sale. People were ready to pay ₹1.5 lakh for it! All his other exhibits had been sold out. On the last day of the exhibition, when Mira and Poncho were helping him disassemble and arrange his things back, a young man in his thirties had tapped Rishi on his shoulder. He had turned to look at a face with a well-trimmed beard and eyes hidden behind blue glasses.

'We have an internship for you. Call me.' A visiting card was held out to him. One side of his lips curved into a perfectly stylish smile. He patted Rishi on the back and threw a quick glance at Mira, before he turned and disappeared into the crowd.

The brother had received many such offers in the last few days. 'Come and learn,' they had said. 'Once you are good enough, we will induct you.'

Rishi had accepted the cards humbly and torn them to pieces after they had left. 'If I am not good enough, then why do you want me? All these beggars want to build their castles on free labour!' he had muttered angrily. At times Mira felt he was being too arrogant. Those were big brands, good names for the CV. Her cousin might just be throwing away opportunities because of his high-headedness. She tried to talk to him about it, very cautiously, taking care that her words were not misplaced or intentions misunderstood. Rishi had curtly stopped her.

'Browny, if I don't respect myself, no one else will. My decisions at this moment might be wrong—maybe mute slavery is indeed the language of the day—but I have to at least try to rise above. I will fight for my self-respect till I can.'

Mira understood where he was coming from. He was not just conflicted about the world, he was deeply hurt by the attitude of his parents. That's where the rebel originated.

She was sure that this new visiting card, too, would land in the dustbin. She went back to the job, but paused when Rishi didn't resume immediately. He was standing still, looking at the card, bewildered.

'Browny, this is Viyaan Iyer!'

'Oh, really?' Mira tried to reciprocate his excitement, though she had no idea who this was. She wondered whether she should ask or just pretend to know. But before she could decide, Rishi ran out of the room, slid through the balcony and rushed down the stairs. Clueless about what might have inspired this reaction, Mira picked up the card that had slipped from his fingers and ran after him. While she huffed and puffed to keep pace with him, she read the name on the card. 'Viyaan M.K. Iyer, Cartoonist and Chief Creative Officer of Buffers Inc.'

There he was, talking to someone under the gulmohar tree.

Rishi rushed downstairs and stopped abruptly, narrowly avoiding bumping into him. Mira, too, was about to collide with Rishi but managed to stop in time. Viyaan Iyer turned. His left hand, with strange beads wrapped around the wrist, went up to push his hair back. The sunglasses came off to reveal amused eyes—half indifferent, half pompous. Rishi stood before him with a hand on his stomach, trying desperately to catch his breath. Viyaan's eyes settled on Mira, frowning at him in disapproval, a few steps behind. He looked back at Rishi.

'Will I be training under you?' Rishi came directly to the point.

'Yes, at ₹20,000 a month. You will be contract-bound with us for a year, failing which…!'

Rishi didn't give him a chance to finish his words. Rishi lunged forward and hugged him. Viyaan Iyer's surprised eyes locked again with the shocked ones of Mira. She wanted to pull him away from this man, smack him on the head, disown him as her cousin. Rishi loosened his grip after a few seconds, now embarrassed with the impulsive display of affection.

'Well,' Viyaan spoke again. 'Anything else?'

Rishi smiled. 'The offer letter, please.'

'Call tomorrow post-lunch.' Viyaan threw his head backwards, shaking his long hair, and walked off.

Rishi watched him go, grinning like an imbecile. Mira punched him when she walked up to him. 'Have you finally gone insane? What do you think you were doing?'

'He is god, Browny! He is to graphics what Kohli is to cricket. The ultimate magician in our trade.'

'Fine.' She was still mad at him. 'But who hugs the person who offers to be your boss? Isn't there something called professional etiquette?'

Rishi grimaced at her and tapped her forehead with his forefinger. 'Those who abide by stupid decorum don't get to train with Viyaan Iyer.' He started walking towards the exhibition hall, whistling a cheap Bollywood track.

'Long hair. Ear studs. Brass kadha on the right hand, beads on the left. Ewwww!' Mira scowled, following him.

The brother looked back at her. 'Had he lifted his T-shirt, you would have seen some mind-boggling tattoos on the man. …But, of course, you don't have a taste for those. You belong to a different era, culturally. You would rather fantasize about a freshly bathed, well-shaven, boring professor with his full-sleeve shirt buttoned right up to his neck, whose wedding proposal would be a numerical puzzle replacing the diamond of the ring to bang your head upon.'

Furious at what Rishi had just said, Mira stopped. Her cousin turned to look at her angry face, laughed and kept walking. She called from behind.

'Is that why you like Virat Kohli so much? Those scary

tattoos that snake around his arm?' she asked sarcastically.

The boy didn't stop. 'Intelligence can invent, Browny; but it takes a rebel to revolutionize.'

'Rebel my foot! Einstein's photographs don't show tattoos. He was rather a well-dressed...!'

Rishi stopped her with a hand up in the air. 'You never know. He may have had some underneath his white shirt. The man did have unruly hair. Why only Einstein? Look at Newton. Pascal. Shakespeare. Michelangelo. Leonardo da Vinci. Rabindranath Tagore. Every great soul who has ever created a stir has had a very avant-garde feel to their appearance. At least none were the short-haired, clean-shaven type. So I won't be surprised if some historian discovers tomorrow that all these people hid their tattoos behind their elaborate attire. Even if they didn't, their handwriting was no less than excellently scripted tattoos on paper.'

Mira's patience had run out. She was about to throw something caustic back at him, when she remembered something and stopped. 'Fine. But how would you get in touch with Tattoo Man to take this revolutionary internship ahead?'

This worked. Rishi stopped dead in his tracks. He spun around, perplexed, and thrust his hands inside his pockets, desperately trying to locate the visiting card Viyaan Iyer had given him. It wasn't there. He looked at Mira, his face pale. The sister revealed the card with a flourish and dramatically blew away imaginary dust off it. Her brother ran after her to grab it.

*

Two days later, when Mira entered college, she carried a box of sweets with her. Her brother had received one of the most prestigious offers in the industry. It was one hell of an achievement to be working with someone he worshipped like God. For once, she wanted to openly flaunt him. Kriti's obsession with Rishi suddenly felt well deserved; so did Rishi's nonchalance of her. She was a proud sister.

She went to all her classmates, trying to include them in the celebration. Kriti placed another piece inside her mouth and leant forward.

'Hey, ask the stud if he'd like to do a photoshoot of me. I think that can break the ice between us. I looooooooove posing for photographs.' Mira looked at her in disbelief, remembering Rishi's forecast a few days back, and burst out laughing. Kriti interpreted her laughter as the perfect response to her drama. But before either could clarify, she snatched the box of sweets and ran outside. Everyone started chasing her, but stopped in their tracks. Kriti was standing in the corridor before Professor Shayan Chatterjee, blocking his path.

'Sir, sweets,' she said. 'Please take some.' She lifted the cover of the box.

Mira couldn't believe what was happening.

'What happened?' The professor raised an eyebrow.

'A dear friend has just landed a fantastic internship with an ad agency. So we are celebrating.'

The professor fished out a sweet and took a bite. He smiled at her, gave her a thumbs up and moved on. Kriti returned to the classroom with a spring in her step; the rest of the girls hurled abuses at her. Only Mira sat resigned, still wondering why she wasn't as smart as Kriti.

In another two hours, the results of the mid-sems were declared. Mira had topped in every paper, except one. She had scored the highest in Digital Message Transmission as well. Professor Chatterjee's research assistant discussed her answers elaborately in class. Feeling shy about the sudden attention, Mira sat in a corner of the class. That day on, she became the professor's favourite.

On the same day, she lost the very first friend she had made in IIT Bombay. Kriti started avoiding her as if she were a criminal.

12.

It was around 6 in the evening when Rishi walked into the plush office of Buffers Inc. He carried his papers in a file. After the regular formalities were done with the HR, the woman heading the department explained his role. He was supposed to work with the creative team in shaping online graphics, packaging, promotions, information graphics and marketing innovations. His participation in brand designing and brand maintenance would be crucial and would impact his performance evaluations.

Rishi asked everything he could to gain clarity about the work and the cultural practices of the organization. He was answered patiently. 'This is a place of fierce passion. The oldest employee in this office is barely 41. Every brainstorming session is about blood and sweat. Decisions are swift, executions swifter. We promise to keep you on your toes.' Rachna, the HR head, passed him a word of caution before he left. 'Don't allow Viyaan's flamboyance to fool you, Rishi. He is one of the most powerful people at Buffers. Even the CEO never challenges his verdict. The other day, he just sent a mail saying he wanted an intern. No one questioned whether we even needed one. When he wants someone out of the system, no one questions that either. He is a person who loves to enjoy life, but when it comes to work, he is ruthless. He must have found you incredibly good to have offered you this internship. But the day he feels you are not working out, it's the end. Our premises have seen many tears.'

'To hell with you!' Rishi muttered under his breath and left her cabin.

He took a turn on his right and then another to reach a big hall, where people sat in small cubicles. From there he took a left to a door that read, 'Viyaan M.K. Iyer.' He knocked. No one responded. He pushed the door open to peep inside and stood rooted. The photograph of Mira on that moonlit night was hung on the wall behind his table.

'Trespassing?'

Rishi spun around.

'You bought that?' he asked, even before he had greeted his new mentor.

'Why else would it be here? That one is the reason you are standing here with me.'

Iyer showed him inside and ordered coffee. 'Your employment here will start mid-summer. That's your college guidelines and our terms put together. Your assignments and holidays shouldn't interrupt your work once you start assisting the team. So you still have four months before joining us. In the meantime, you are free to come over and spend time with the team and figure out how things happen here.'

Rishi listened intently. Frequently, he glanced at the huge frame on the wall. Somehow, the image of his sister hanging in the cabin of his new boss felt unsettling. What bothered him more was Viyaan's strange appreciation of it. *That one is the reason you are standing here with me.*

Out on the Bandra Kurla Complex (BKC), he walked aimlessly along the footpath and passed the overcrowded bus stops. He bumped into a few pedestrians by accident. Some of them advised him to keep his eyes open; others just assumed he was drunk. He wasn't listening to any of them. And then it dawned on him.

Am I getting overprotective? The girl in the photograph was no more than a model for Viyaan. He lived in the company of the most striking women in society. It was too absurd that he was suddenly floored by his sister's face, so much so that he had bought her photograph and hung it on the wall of his office!

Finally, he smiled. But yes, his possessiveness for his sister and her emotional dependence on him would need a serious trimming.

BKC to Powai would be a tiring journey during the peak hours of traffic. He grimaced and hired a cab. By the time he got home, it was quite late. He saw the sister sulking. She was writing on her notepad.

'What is troubling you?' he asked.

'Kriti,' she answered sadly. 'She did not even congratulate me.'

'Oh, come on, Browny. Toppers don't have friends.' Rishi dismissed her melancholy.

'But she is nice. People in college talk to me because they want to spend time with her,' she almost cried.

'Stop being a crybaby.' Rishi made a face. His sudden rudeness unsettled her and she looked up at him.

'Browny, didn't I tell you right at the beginning that she isn't with you for friendship? She wanted you for company. She needed some kind of follower who wouldn't threaten her existence. She is this glamorous charmer who can naturally attract attention. You were the perfect follower for her, because you wouldn't ever try to be like her. She treated you as that "anonymous friend to the heroine", and you allowed her to do that. By scoring higher than everyone else in class, you have violated an unspoken agreement between the two of you. That didn't work with her!'

Mira continued to look at him. His words were the least flattering, but she knew they were true. Kriti did treat her as the unsmart, second-class woman who was supposed to be graced by her presence. Mira ignored her vanity because she didn't have a choice.

Rishi smiled. Of all the issues on earth, his cousin was sulking about the disappearance of a non-existent friendship! After dinner, he asked whether she wanted to go for a late-night drive. 'Those who don't have hope still have Kohli!' He pointed at his bike keys. His sister rolled her eyes. They stopped at a pub a few miles from home. The music was deafening. They picked a table outside in the open air.

Rishi smiled at her. 'Relax, Browny. Loosen up a little. For how long do you want to play the small-town-girl? It doesn't work.' Mira was turning pale with every word. 'What I mean is, you have all the qualities to be a fantasy woman. Just that you have to know that you are one. You make heads turn. Why are you feeding this lack of confidence?'

He remembered the photograph hanging on Viyaan Iyer's wall. A face that could arouse the interest of a genius didn't deserve to be isolated and dependent. Who the hell was this stupid Kriti to dump her? Rishi felt a surge of irritation. 'What was the effect of your results on the Why-Aren't-You-Studying guy?'

The question was sudden. Mira's expression changed. The

professor had openly declared how happy he was with her paper. She smiled.

'Look at yourself,' the brother said. 'If you were smart enough, that weird golden spectacle would have been in your pocket by now. But you don't want to try. Why don't you shed your inhibitions and flaunt your goodness? The point is, you are one of the most interesting women around. It's so innocent of you to not be aware of it. But at least don't think that you are not.'

Rishi's words would continue to echo in her mind even after that evening was long gone. Late at night when she couldn't sleep, in front of the bathroom mirror, while walking along the corridors of her college and while looking at Kriti—as usual the centre of attention and commotion—from afar.

Professor Shayan Chatterjee had selected her as an associate for a project he was supervising on behalf of a telecom company. This meant she now had direct access to his cabin. She would also be doing her thesis under him. Stealthily, at times, she looked at him. He was as distant as he had always been, but selecting her from among a bunch of students was a strong statement affirming his fondness. She tried to imagine him standing somewhere for her with roses one day and chuckled. Shayan looked up to see what was funny. She shuffled around some papers with a serious expression on her face. The professor went back to work. Mira had no idea whether he had a girlfriend. Did he only have overenthusiastic girls writing ballads for him on campus—ballads that never reached him? But was he romantic? Mira again glanced at him. Once again, Rishi's words from that night reverberated in her mind.

'You will pass out of college, get a fantastic job, make

money, get married, have kids, raise them and die one day. All without knowing that you could have been someone's fantasy woman. You could be the poetry in someone's music. Break the shell, Browny. Do it.'

She didn't understand all of it, but what Rishi had said was beautiful. A new person she didn't seem to know much about had raised its head inside her. For the first time, between her work and studies, she was thinking about herself.

Problem No. 3,297: ME!

13.

That evening Mira leisurely walked towards Kunj Bihari's tea stall. A few people were already there, chatting and laughing. Rishi hadn't yet reached. Two of the men were senior professors. They were discussing the technical issues of e-commerce. She sat down quietly and smiled at Kunj Bihari. The old man passed her a cup.

'Waiting for brother?' he asked, revealing the betel stains on his teeth. She nodded.

'Very fine boy. Every time he sits here with my tea, I find a few girls hovering around for his attention. He never responds. But they buy my tea.'

Mira wondered if that was why he found Rishi a 'very fine boy'! Or was it the tips he left him?

'My old eyes have seen so many boys and girls coupling up on the campus. Over my cups of tea, they sing songs of spring. Then they have ugly break-ups. They shamelessly turn up a few days later with different partners. Sometimes even professors play these love games. These days no one has any sense of ethics. No profession is noble, no student cares about limits!' He was on a rant, but Mira interrupted him.

'Professors too?' she asked, shocked. 'Who?'

The old man quickly lowered his voice, rolled his eyes and whispered how a professor in the past had two-timed students. 'But I suspected right from the beginning,' he added. 'The rascal put the two girls in two different groups, and when one of the girls would be working on her practicals, he would be romancing the other. He told both the girls to keep a low profile about their affair, because otherwise the authorities would separate the lovebirds.' The old man's eyes grew wider by the minute. 'And guess what, after he ditched both and left for New York, the girls fought like cats and dogs here at my stall, sitting on this very bench.' He motioned to where Mira was sitting. Uncomfortable immediately, Mira got up to change her seat and bumped into someone behind her, stumbling back to the same place. Embarrassed, she looked up at the one she may have offended. The man looked familiar. Before she could utter an apology, he asked, 'Gossiping about professors?'

Taken aback by this sudden, intrusive allegation, Mira fumbled, 'No, not at all...I mean, of course not!' The man sat down on the opposite bench.

'But you were listening to gossip. That's equally bad.'

Irritated at this interference, she looked away. Kunj Bihari was now focused on the tea boiling in the saucepan before him, like a scientist awaiting his eureka moment. Where the hell was Rishi? She checked her watch.

'So you are a student here?' the man asked. He seemed to have found her nervous recoil funny. Mira nodded like it could mean a yes, or a no, or a maybe, or a very good. She tried to concentrate on the cup of tea in her hand, or the contents of her bag, the banyan tree in front, the clouds above, her unruly hair—anything that could make her ignore this intrusive man sitting opposite her and staring strangely. He was leaning forward, his elbow supported on his knee. The short kurta he wore hung loose, revealing a considerable part of his chest. Her frowns and deep show of concentrating on the tea didn't have any effect on his shameless, unapologetic and amused gaze. She wanted to get up and leave, when her eye caught something dark peeping out from under the left hem of his unbuttoned kurta. It seemed part of a design with a nicely crafted motif radiating from a circle.

Was that a tattoo? The man in front followed her gaze to the exposed area of his chest. He straightened up and pulled down the neckline of his kurta to one side, now clearly revealing his chest. 'It's a sun tattoo,' he said. 'A tribal design. Got it made in Goa last year. Nice?'

Eyes wide, vocabulary forgotten, Mira wished she could disappear. Shocked and red with embarrassment, she now realized who this man was. The longish hair, the tiny stud on the left ear, the tattoo on the chest. This was Rishi's Tattoo Man. He was the one who had offered her brother his dream internship, flaunting which she had distributed sweets in her college. She just couldn't place his name. She wanted to give him an earful and run. But this was her cousin's new boss. 'I have to leave,' she got up.

He showed no signs of having heard her. 'How do you know Rishi?'

'He's my first cousin,' Mira reported meekly, standing up and slinging her bag on her shoulder.

'Heyyy!' A loud, cheerful tone sounded from somewhere. 'How come you are here?'

Mira was relieved that her brother had reached. She couldn't tolerate this man any longer. Tattoo Man told Rishi that he came here sometimes—two of the professors were his batch mates from school. Also, there were projects he worked on with IIT Bombay. And that he was quite surprised to spot Mira there. Neither of them seemed to be in any mood to leave. Mira excused herself. 'I'll see you in the library, Rishi,' she declared before leaving.

Rishi watched her go. Her sudden retreat couldn't be a coincidence. He turned to face Viyaan. 'What have you done to her?' he asked directly.

Viyaan shrugged. 'I found her peeping at my tattoo, so I just pulled my kurta aside to make it visible, and told her it's a sun.'

A few minutes passed in utter silence. Then, abruptly, both burst out laughing, making some of the tea spill from Kunj Bihari's startled hands.

'Please, man! She is way too innocent for such pranks.' The brother said, still laughing.

'I couldn't stop myself, bro,' Viyaan laughed back. 'So straight. Her disapprovals are written on her face. She was perhaps wondering why my kind of species even exists! She kept stealing glances at me to reassure herself that her judgement was right.' He laughed again. 'No wonder she made for a brilliant photography subject.'

This reference pricked Rishi again, and this time he put it across bluntly. 'Why did you say that you wanted me as an intern because of that frame?'

Viyaan looked at him, his eyes suddenly sharp. 'I didn't mean it to be my way of getting access to your cousin. I was talking about the work.' He turned suddenly, to find Kunj Bihari feeding on every word hungrily, perhaps gathering meat for his next gossip. Viyaan glared at him and the man immediately looked away, pretending to occupy himself with washing utensils.

He looked back at Rishi and the amusement was back on his face. 'Don't blame me if this level of entertainment tempts me out of my ethics.' A few birds chirruped in protest and the other customers at the stall turned to locate the source of the resounding laughter that came from the tea stall that tired evening.

*

Mira was left with a hammering inside her head as she sat in the library. God! What was she thinking, staring at his chest like that? And why did that terrible man have to spot her doing that? She wanted to dissolve into thin air. He must be thinking that she was a hopelessly frustrated woman. She took out as many books as she could, placed them on the table and hid behind them, so no one knew she was there. The brother found her anyway. 'Now I know why Mr Go-To-Your-Class is so scared of his students,' he said and got slapped. She tried to explain herself, but Rishi stopped her with a pat on the shoulders. 'It's okay, Browny.'

'No, it's not. I behaved like a pervert!' She felt silly. 'I didn't mean to do that. I was just…'

'Trust me, Browny,' he assured. 'The man has gone through a lot of pain and spent a lot of money to get that tattoo made. You ogling at it is value for money. So it's fine.'

Mira tried her best to believe him, but couldn't. For the next few days, she kept feeling that everyone knew what had happened at Kunj Bihari's stall. Everyone who looked at her seemed to snigger at her actions. She avoided the tea stall as if there was a monster waiting there. When Shayan Chatterjee called her to take an update on the project, she thought he would scold her for peeping into Viyaan's kurta. He didn't. Every time Kriti looked at her sarcastically, she feared she would announce to the world that Professor Chatterjee's 'favourite' was stealing peeks at the chest of a Virat Kohli-tattoo lookalike. Unmindfully, one evening, she had even typed a Facebook status on why she found tattoos meaningless. When Rishi was the first person to 'like' the status, she deleted it.

One day when no one was around, she typed in 'Viyaan Iyer' on Google. It immediately threw up a lot of interviews and reports, along with images of him and his works. The interviews said he was Tamil, born and brought up in Bengaluru. In only eight years, he had travelled across the world working with leading dailies and two of the best ad agencies in the world, created lampoon-like cartoons and fantastic jingles, punchlines, print ads and ad films, launched campaigns, built brands across countries, won national and international awards, and made for himself a profile that was fascinating and enviable. No wonder Rishi had said the other day that he was even willing to be his pet cat, if not an intern.

She browsed through his works available on Google. Some of the best ads of the time were his creations. His portfolio included the image of a nude woman seated on crystals, her hair falling in front. Faintly, she remembered that this one had made for endless debate on social media a year or two back because of the controversy the rudraksh around the woman's bare waist had created. Many political and religious wings had shunned the art and its creator; their supporters had hurled abuses at him and threatened him of dire consequences. But when the piece of art was awarded The Hugo Boss Prize in the United States, the same people changed their stand overnight and started showering him with praise for bringing such pride to the country.

Viyaan Iyer looked different then, with short hair and a stubble.

14.

Rishi got home very late that evening. His classes were over early and he had gone to Buffers after that. Viyaan had instructed him that within a month's time, he should tell him his specific areas of interest within the creative offers at the organization. This meant he had only a month to understand what happened in which corner of the four-storey building at BKC. Since he hadn't joined formally, it was up to him how he managed his time, built his relationships, convinced people to cooperate and came back with relevant insights. Interacting with the teams, spending time in multiple cubicles and finally making way through the crazy Mumbai traffic took a lot of time. He tried to be as quiet as possible when he opened the door and took off his shoes. Mira had slept, but she groggily lifted herself on the bed and waited as Rishi placed his watch on the rack.

'Go back to sleep,' he said affectionately.

She wanted to, but her eye had caught something peeping out from his open bag. 'What's that?' she asked.

'I think he has started liking you.'

'Who?' She sat up straight in bed, her sleep gone.

'Viyaan, who else?' Rishi blurted.

'Why? He has inked my name on his right chest?' she asked sarcastically.

'No. Not yet.' Rishi laughed. 'Here.'

A gift-wrapped box came flying towards her. She caught it and took the cover off with a lot of care. She folded it neatly and tucked it under the mattress. Her brother laughed again. 'You typical cheapo. Now you will use that wrapper for someone else.'

'Better to keep stuff handy. You never know when you need what!' She turned her concentration to the box. Inside was a pretty red mug with beautiful block prints on it and a little teddy with a pink satin sash around its neck. Hanging from one side of the mug was a tiny white card that read, 'Peace!'

Mira held the mug and the teddy in her hands. Thin lines appeared on her forehead. Rishi studied her reactions keenly. She looked up. 'What does this mean? Why did he send me these?'

'Because his name is scripted in gold in the list of ten biggest flirts in the world,' he mumbled, to which his sister impatiently explained she would appreciate it if he were louder. 'Well, either he likes me a little too much, which is unlikely, or he likes you, which is quite possible. Else, this means no more than him trying to make up for the embarrassment he may have caused you.' Rishi poured himself a glass of water.

'So what do I do with these now?' She looked up, confused.

'You decide. It's your call.'

'It's my call?' she asked anxiously. 'Won't you be affected by my call? What if I don't want to accept these?'

'Treat yourself as a separate human being, Browny. This gesture is personal. Viyaan's association with me is professional. He is shrewd enough and I am ambitious enough, not to mix the two. But it's not about us. It's about you. First decide what you want to do; later we'll decide what you should do.'

He slid into the bathroom to wash up. Mira got up to lay out dinner.

As Rishi ate the chapatis hungrily, the sister still looked confused. With his mouth full, he gestured with his hands for her to tell him what was going on.

'You didn't ask him why...?' She was expecting her cousin to help her sort this out. She looked at the mug. It was nice. And the teddy really cute.

'No,' said the brother. 'But you're thinking too much.' He paused for a sip of water. 'The man's perspective is, he felt he had offended you; so this is his way of calling for truce. You might wonder why he'd be bothered at all. But people do take note of these things and react. That's the goodness of being. Maybe someone else would have apologized right there. Maybe some other person wouldn't have cared. Viyaan wanted it this way. Nothing more.'

Mira seemed to like that answer. She was now busy cuddling the teddy. Rishi gathered the dishes and put them in the kitchen sink. As he wiped his mouth, he looked at her again. What he had told her was comforting. But the waters seemed deeper. Viyaan had very casually handed over the parcel to him. He had said that it was a 'no hard feelings, buddy' gift for Mira. Rishi's intuition said he would look for more excuses to meet her. He didn't know whether that was good or bad. He could impress without meaning a thing! Viyaan wasn't a poetic sort of guy who would sit by the river and count ripples. He was the horse that galloped his way through thorns. He didn't wait for things to happen; he made things happen. That was a characteristic that they both shared. This was probably why he was fond of Rishi. On the flip side, Viyaan wasn't as patient as him. He wanted results at a furious pace, always keen to move on.

'Approach your task like a tiger and rip it apart till you have fed yourself on it,' he had told Rishi a few days back. 'That hunger is important. The day you lose that, you are of no use.' The point was, would Mira be able to deal with this kind of madness? He had decided, though, that he wouldn't interfere. He had to let them figure this out.

Is she still infatuated with that Go-To-Your-Class professor? What a vast difference there was between the personalities of Shayan Chatterjee and Viyaan Iyer, he chuckled as he thought to himself. One was a reluctant saint; the other was known to break hearts. One was reserved; the other was bubbling with energy. One was persistent; the other was passionate. One attracted women; the other scared them. One kept women at bay; the other flirted openly.

Rishi frowned. God knows what Viyaan was thinking. He could be a dangerous man to date, but he wasn't evil. Rishi had tried to dig up as much on him as he could, to understand what kind of corporate politics Viyaan tended to play and to check his equation with the women around. He learnt that the ad man was a hard taskmaster and an irresistible charmer, but he wasn't a perpetual offender.

He was now lying on the floor and frowning at the ceiling, when a strange sound from the bed stemmed his flow of thoughts. He sat up.

'Browny, why are you laughing?'

Mira was lying on her back, her right hand holding the teddy and the left on her stomach, trying hard to control herself. Her eyes were watering and she was finding it difficult to speak. Between gasps and peals of laughter, she managed to utter a few disconnected words, while softly poking the teddy with her finger.

'Motilal…you and Sunny…remember? Motilal?'

She didn't have to finish; Rishi was already on the floor, laughing with his face buried in the pillow.

Many years ago, Rishi had carried a large teddy bear with him to Shimla during the summer holidays. Little Mira was hooked to the soft toy. Rishi preferred listening to ghost stories from Shiraz.

'It walks when everyone has fallen asleep,' Rishi had told Sunny one night, pointing to the large brown teddy. 'Motilal, the milk man, was killed by a giant bear at Narkanda many years ago. No one came to save him when the bear threw him off the hills. So now, after death, Motilal enters big houses and makes them his own. You will hear him coughing, laughing, talking and walking around all night when everyone has fallen asleep.'

That night Sunny couldn't sleep. He almost heard echoing voices and resounding laughter outside, as the wind howled and blew through the open terrain, hitting the pitch dark mountains at night, to create the strangest of noises. When a few utensils fell off the kitchen shelf, he covered himself with a shawl and started chanting the Hanuman Chalisa loud enough to wake up Saundarya. The terrified rants on the days that followed left the entire family laughing for months!

'Poor Sunny!' Rishi's eyes had gone red with tears of laughter.

Moments of silence followed. Both were lost in the fading images of a childhood bungalow that transformed into a fairytale destination every summer. The kitchen would be active all day.

Someone or the other would always come to meet them. They would go to local fairs and temples and gardens.

Mira crawled to the edge of the bed and looked down at Rishi, suddenly excited. 'Come to Shimla this summer. Deepti Bua won't know. No one will know. Not even dad. I'll tell him that you are the son of a professor and that you are in town for a project. Please come. You will love it. Will you?'

She was saying all this so earnestly, Rishi glanced at her. 'I don't know, Browny. But this summer, something will change. Things will not remain this way; we will no longer hide that we are both in Mumbai, staying together in an apartment.' He looked away, stared at the ceiling and spoke, almost to himself, 'We will hatch a plan and make this happen. We have lost enough, all of us. We will clear the mess up this summer.'

15.

Rishi was busy working with Poncho on the outer wall of an old-age home in Ville Parle. The government had undertaken a campaign for Beautiful Maharashtra; all big brands had been quick to harness this for their CSR activities. A paint company had added 'Colourful Maharashtra' as a prefix to its name, in acknowledgement of the Beautiful Maharashtra initiative. This meant some extra bucks for Rishi and an excuse to stay out of class for Poncho. A lot of work had to be completed before Holi. Rishi was trying to work out a schedule for the tight deadline when his phone beeped. He ignored it. After a few seconds it beeped again. And then again. Poncho sighed.

'God knows when women will be as desperate for me too.'

Rishi took his phone out. There were three messages from Mira.

'Thanks for the mug and the teddy.'

'Hey, thanks. They are cute.'

'Thanks for the gift. But you shouldn't have bothered.'

He dialled her number. 'What are you doing, Browny?'

'Hey, which of these is cool and won't mean that I am interested or anything?' She sounded anxious.

'All of them show that your brain is hibernating.'

'What!' Mira yelled from the other end. 'I am just cooking up a neutral thanks message.'

Rishi wiped his sweat with a handkerchief. There isn't a spring in Mumbai. February mornings are hot. 'Awesome! But who on earth sits and wonders what message leaves what impression—that, too, on someone you haven't even met properly? Say thanks if you have to. Or don't. Who cares?'

Meekly, Mira tried to explain. But Rishi knew it already. This was her general attitude towards life. It was not just about sending Viyaan a reply. It was her innate need to be perfect all the time.

He turned to find Poncho briskly drawing some geometric shapes. He quietly picked up his brush to add texture to them. As his fingers worked, his mind wandered somewhere far away, among lush terrain, small tiled houses, simple people and cold breeze. This summer, it would be Mission Shimla.

At home, Mira kept her phone back in her bag. 'True. Why do I care?'

'How can I not? For the first time a man has given me a gift! Something that Kriti never fails to flaunt—every single purse or perfume she receives from her admirers. Of course, Viyaan isn't an admirer. But then, how do I interpret this? What would dad say if he knew?'

'Rishi thinks I am walking on the edge of desperation.'

'I am just...'

The debate between her rational self and her restless brain seemed unending.

She didn't like the man, right?

Or did she, secretly?

'Of course not!' the rational brain screamed. 'It's just that receiving an unexpected gift from an attractive man feels adventurous, different.'

'Attractive?' the restless brain laughed.

'Well, thick eyebrows, nasty eyes, mischievous grin! When he stared at me, something churned inside. As if my eyes, my hair, my face were being evaluated—no, appreciated.'

Random questions had been lurking in her mind for the past few days. She wanted to ignore them and move on, but they kept coming back whenever she was idle. She shook her head in an attempt to brush off the thoughts of this strange man and smiled at Kunj Bihari.

'You and your brother have forgotten me, Mira Didi,' Kunj Bihari complained.

'No, Kunj Bihariji. My brother has taken up some work, so he can't come here every day. And I have to get the laundry and grocery shopping done, since he doesn't have too much time now. I have my assignments too.' Mira smiled at his unhappy face.

'I understand all of that, Mira Didi. But do take some time out for this old man. I feel nice when I see you two—reminds me of my grandchildren back home in my village. They are young now, but someday they will grow up to go to a nice big college like you two.' He exposed his betel-stained teeth again and added a few pieces of cardamom to the tea. Those were special offers from him to customers he liked.

Mira smiled at the aroma of the boiling tea. Kunj Bihari wondered if he could sell her some of those cakes lying unsold since last week. He cleared his throat to embark on a sales pitch, when he spotted someone walking their way in long strides. He groaned inwardly. This man acted too smart. He didn't like him. He wanted to warn Mira, but before he could open his mouth, the man opened his.

'Hi. What's up?' That enquiry was obviously for Mira. He sat himself down on the bench, threw his head backwards and inhaled deeply.

Mira almost dropped her cup of tea at this sudden, unexpected company. She composed herself, hesitated and managed to smile back. 'Hi.'

'All good? Your M.Tech has something to do with terrible tea? I always find you here,' he said, as he folded the sleeves of his shirt, thrown on casually over a pair of low-waist jeans.

Kunj Bihari scowled. The joker was trying to take his customers away. He was also bad-mouthing his tea! He never boiled the same tea leaves as many times as they did at the college canteen.

Mira had almost started to explain that her classes had just got over and that she had come here for a breather, but she paused. 'That's better than staying away from the office that pays for getting expensive tattoos inked. No?'

Absolutely. Fantastic. Well served. Kunj Bihari wanted to give the girl a standing ovation. The silly man smiled, but didn't order a cup of tea for himself yet. Should he ask him to leave the bench and his customer alone, if he did not want to place an order?

'No,' the old man thought. 'You never know who comes with what contacts. Why make enemies unnecessarily?' The idiot was still sitting there, smiling at the innocent girl. Her eyes shifted nervously, unable to find the appropriate words to either end or entertain the man's gaze. She looked hesitant; the man confident. He didn't seem to know that anything that happened here could only happen over Kunj Bihari's tea. He cleared his throat and prepared to ask whether he could serve him a cup, but stopped, shocked, as he heard Mira saying, 'Thanks for the gift. The teddy was very cute, and the mug... Rishi said the prints on the mug were your design. Is that true? They are beautiful.'

Oh my God! There was a history here! Something new was happening on campus and Kunj Bihari had no clue! That was absurd. He chose not to interrupt, and listen. He poured some of the hot tea in a glass and kept it on the bench next to the man. There was no refusal from him. Now he would get to charge him anyway.

'I just felt that acting smart with a pretty woman might cost me more than it should,' Viyaan unmindfully lifted the cup, took a sip, winced and looked at Kunj Bihari, only to catch him ogling at them. The old man quickly tried to shift his gaze, but it was too late.

Mira saw Viyaan's reaction to the taste of the tea. 'You have to specifically ask him to put less sugar, otherwise...' she shrugged. Tattoo Man stopped looking angrily at Kunj Bihari and turned to face her. 'Listen,' he said. 'For three nights I have worked non-stop without sleep. I badly want to declutter and spend time with someone who knows nothing about my work. If you are too busy, then may I ask this weird old man to come with me for a coffee with less sugar?'

Mira's breath caught in her throat. Was he really asking her out? She didn't want to say no. She looked at her watch. 'I'll get my bag and laptop,' she paid for the tea and walked away.

So his assumption was right—this man was trying to shoo away his customers! Kunj Bihari was enraged. Every year there were always some jokers like this one who tried to throw him out of business. But there was God; He would protect him.

He looked up at the sky and touched his forehead with the tip of his fingers. The man on the bench looked at his watch repeatedly. Kunj Bihari tried to start a conversation. 'Should I make you another cup of tea? This time with less sugar? Actually, students here go through very grinding schedules. The extra dose of sugar cheers them up, you see.'

The check-shirt's angry eyes fell on him like the mace of an angry Bhima. They showed no respect for his attempts to revoke lost trust. He looked at his watch again.

'She'll take time. She'll have to seek permission from Shayan Sir before leaving the premises. Shayan Sir is very strict. Mira Didi is his favourite student. She likes him a lot. They are together most of the time on campus. So she will take time to show up here. She won't step out unless he permits. You do have time for another cup. This time it will be less sugar, I promise,' the old man said, nodding wisely.

Viyaan's eyes narrowed at him. This piece of crap was trying to feed him nonsense. How on earth did the people here tolerate him? He got up and paced up and down restlessly, waiting for Mira to get back.

She appeared eventually, and the two left the campus. Kunj Bihari watched them go. So here starts another story! He had seen enough on this campus to know which ones would end up as a short story and which ones would become a novel. This didn't seem like it would be a short story. But it certainly was a bad story. He didn't like this long-haired man. Too much of a mismatch for Mira Didi. He smiled to himself. If not anything else, he had managed to plant a seed of jealousy in the mind of this man who said his tea was not good. Now he would try to find out who Shayan Chatterjee was and what he meant to Mira. Kunj Bihari remembered the disgust and curiosity in the man's eyes when he was told about Mira's fondness for the professor. He'd ask stupid questions now, suspect that Mira was having a scene inside campus; he'd instruct her to stay away from Chatterjee; she wouldn't; they'd fight; and then they'd break up. Sorted!

Kunj Bihari could see the future as if it were a film playing out before him. Mira Didi deserved better. He decided to talk about this to her brother.

It was pack-up time for Rishi and Poncho. With a wet towel they wiped the colours that stained their hands and clothes. Exhausted, they lay down flat on the footpath, as the sun, even at 6 p.m., showed no signs of toning down the blaze.

'Rishi, don't you think pearl is not the right colour for the patch there?' Poncho made an observation.

Rishi also felt the same. He stared at it. 'What do you suggest?' he asked.

Poncho thought for a while. 'Remember the laddoos Aunty brought with her when she visited Mumbai once? That kind of cream.'

Rishi laughed. This foodie loved to describe everything through food. He sobered up immediately. His mother had come to Mumbai only once after his admissions. She called at times, but the conversations were short. She had no idea what was happening in his life. He had tried to tell her initially, but when she didn't seem interested, he had stopped.

'Whatever makes you happy,' she'd say with a sigh. Yes,

Rishi was happy. But why wasn't she happy for him?

'Let's go with the laddoo cream then. Tomorrow,' Rishi said, distracting himself from his thoughts. He got up and picked up the keys to his bike. His phone beeped with a message from Mira.

'Tattoo Man at our tea stall. Wants to have coffee outside,' it read.

'Have fun. Call me if you need anything.' He sent her a reply and sat on his bike.

'Kohli, it's been a tough day, mate. Way too much to do. Those guys at Buffers are after my life, asking me to submit the list I want to work on by this weekend. There are also pending assignments in college. Will take a while to finish this wall and move on to the next. Also, gotta plan the summers. Too little time, too much work. Say something, dude, what do I do?'

The engine roared.

Rishi looked around from behind the visor. The city lights were coming on. The girl from his class who had been hitting on him till a while back was now hanging around with another guy. She smiled at him seductively from the distance, perhaps trying to keep her options open. He looked away. These lights, the crowd, the chaos—they always told him that there was hope beyond the melancholy. Mumbai has a kind of ruthless energy that runs like blood in the veins of its residents. The city acts as a leveller and gets everyone to run to its own rhythm. Everyone learns to come to terms with the unruly commands of the city. Hadn't Mira, too, changed since she had come here? She used to be so shy, and today, she was out on her first date. Well, something like a date, because for the first time she had gone out with someone other than Rishi.

He stopped at the next signal and looked around. He had a little friend here who sold incense sticks. He couldn't see him, but in a short while, he felt a weight on his pillion seat. He turned to take a look. The dark boy with unkempt hair and oversized clothes, barely a teenager, flashed him a smile. Rishi smiled back from behind his helmet.

'How many did you sell today?' he asked.

'Only nine packets left,' the boy said proudly.

At the next signal, Rishi dropped him off, not before buying the rest of his incense packets. The boy thanked him, beaming. Rishi took off his helmet to feel the breeze. The young boy looked at his face and asked, 'You look tired. What happened?'

'Just occupied with a lot of things. You won't understand.' Rishi almost dismissed him.

'Tell me. You never know.' The boy smiled mischievously.

'Well,' Rishi said, 'My cousin and I are planning our summer holidays. Our parents have not been on talking terms for a while now, and we want to make peace between them. We want to be able to go to each other's place again and enjoy like a big family, like we used to. Do you have a solution for this?' He watched the boy, waiting for him to say that he couldn't solve others' family issues. But what he said left him frozen. And Rishi flashed him his eureka smile.

'Do what you just said—go to each other's place,' the boy said, before disappearing into the crowd.

16.

'Rishi is very fond of you.' Mira tried to start a conversation.

'And you are not!' Viyaan sipped his coffee, amused eyes lingering on Mira. From her face they came down to her hands, nervously hugging a cushion to her chest, and went back to settle on her face. The girl was stiff. Her fingers were now restlessly fidgeting with the tassels of the cushion. He spent a fraction of a second examining the tense fingers. Not manicured, no fancy nail paint—non-committedly bare!

Watching him observing her fingers, Mira quickly slid them behind the cushion, as if they had been caught committing a crime. The only good it led to was Viyaan's eyes going back to rest on her face.

'So, other than those in your college and at home, who are you fond of?' he asked finally.

'Shah Rukh Khan.' Mira grinned as if she was sitting with the actor and not Viyaan.

The eyebrows in front raised and dropped. 'Okay. I get it.' He looked frustrated. 'You like people who make strange sounds when they laugh. Every time he laughs during our shoots, the crew gets scared thinking that's a machine gun firing.'

Mira wanted to protest. God knew why most men enjoyed taking nasty digs at Shah Rukh Khan. She asked instead, 'Rishi told me you are a renowned cartoonist. Then what are you doing with Shah Rukh Khan?'

'Why, you didn't know?' he almost spat out. The 'Rishi told me' part didn't go down well with him. What did she mean? His illustrations still appeared in leading dailies, magazines and websites. There's no reason why someone should act so naïve. Quite unlike him, he swallowed this bout of displeasure. The innocent face looked back at him pleasantly, unaware of his brazen ego. He couldn't bring himself to crush the simplicity sparkling in those large, beautiful eyes with his impulsive brashness. Instead, he looked outside the window and shrugged.

'Well, we can't be the same person, doing the same things all our life. I get bored very fast. I am popular as a cartoonist, true, but after three years of doing that with a daily, I wanted to learn more. Buffers exploits me very well. Today I have more to offer as a digital artist.'

Mira didn't quite know what it was to be bored of life. For her, life was a journey that was meant to be lived the way it was. She had accepted things without complaint. After all, what would change even if she didn't? And if nothing would change, then why try at all?

She made a mental note. Problem No. 3,300: Try to change life or let it be?

She glanced at Viyaan. He had bent forward, with his elbows supported on his knees, palms covering his mouth, looking at her. 'What were you thinking?' he asked.

'Can you really take control of your life? There's something called destiny too…'

'Losers give in to destiny. Others write their own.' Viyaan leant forward a little more. 'It's destined that at times my wicked humour will piss you off. But this evening, us sitting together over coffee, is the version of destiny I scripted myself.' He found Mira blushing and straightened up. 'Life is speed, Mira. In this short span of life, aren't we all running to grab all that we can? At this speed, the sooner we know what works for us, the more we are sorted.'

Mira nodded. Rishi knew what was right for him. Viyaan knew. Only she didn't. 'You are so much like Rishi,' she murmured.

'Rishi,' the cartoonist smiled. 'Yes, we do share some complex traits. It was important that we get together to string those. Your brother's right brain is a trap. His concepts are often better than mine.'

'What!' Mira couldn't contain herself. 'He worships you. How would he...!'

Viyaan cut her short. 'I know he does. But his creative sense is phenomenal. In fact, his ideas and foresight are way better than what I had when I was a student.' He looked at Mira. 'Remember that image of yours he displayed at the exhibition? It was about a simple girl looking out of the window on a moonlit night. But he had the wisdom to read more into that; he transported it to a different world altogether. He made me feel that there would be a void in my artsy treasure if I didn't own that piece.'

Mira felt her heart swell with pride. She wanted to hug her cousin.

'That work is a strong story, a brilliant one. And an insufficient one.'

Mira's smile faded. 'Why insufficient?'

'Insufficient because...' he smiled. 'Don't get me wrong here, Mira. But it is insufficient because my appreciation for that image did not end with the image. It urged me to know more about the girl in it. He made me fall in love.'

Mira stiffened. Viyaan noticed the redness in her face. 'It is that insufficiency that hooks the audience. Your brother knows how to punch that code of insufficiency into his work and tease his audience with the absence of something that's as vast as nature, but not quite within their grasp.'

Mira lifted her eyes to find Viyaan playing with her keys. He stopped and held it out for her. They sat quietly for a while before he spoke again. 'He has a complicated brain, your cousin. He thought I bought the frame because I was trying to hit on you.'

Mira smiled. 'He is a protective brother with high self-esteem. At times I end up saying or doing things that hurt him. I don't know how to mend those,' she said unmindfully.

'Don't even try. You will mess it up more,' Viyaan warned her. 'Artists are sentimental people. And this one, your brother, is a very weird character. He would probably even walk out of my office if he is convinced that I am interested in you as a model more than in him as an artist.' He paused. 'But Rishi deserves a platform, and the mentoring that comes with it. Sentimental people are vulnerable, ending up in the wrong hands if they are unhappy. His talent needs that protection and conservation.'

Of course they do. Mira remembered how uncomfortable she felt every time Rishi spoke of his friends smoking weed. God knew which breed Viyaan was! Success is a different breed altogether, she argued with herself and looked back at him. 'Why are you telling me all this?'

Viyaan was perhaps expecting that question. 'As far as I

have understood, Rishi's philosophy of life is woven around you. You are his weakness. The day you become his strength, he will become a force to be reckoned with. I thought I must tell you.'

Mira had mixed feelings about everything she was hearing. She was puzzled. She could figure that Viyaan was spending time with her for a reason. The reason seemed noble. Yet confusing. But he meant well. Meekly, she asked, 'How can I help?'

'We will figure that out.' Tattoo Man smiled reassuringly as he stood up to leave.

When she came back home that evening, Rishi was in a deep sleep. She looked at his handsome face. Pride coursed through her again. Her idiot brother was destined to rule the world.

Next morning she received an image on WhatsApp from an unknown number. It showed an animated image of Shah Rukh Khan holding a rose for Mira. She giggled at the way her face and Shah Rukh's were distorted, with a longer nose, bigger eyes and bulging cheeks. A voice from behind her made her look away from the screen.

'Someone seems to have made peace with tattoos.'

Mira handed Rishi the phone. He looked at it with a frown and threw it back on the bed. 'This is what happens when you spend time with a woman. You waste yourself on nonsense just to please her.'

Mira made a face at him.

'Thank you. I am elated. But Rishi feels I made you waste precious time,' she typed in the reply and sent it with an emoticon.

Pat came the response. 'He is right. I was up till late for work; did this after I was done and dead tired.'

'Why?' she typed back.

No response.

Mira kept the phone away. Cheeky guy. But she was enjoying the attention. Life suddenly seemed interesting. She dug her face into the pillow. The brother's probing eyes were not something she wanted right now. He'd just tear her away from this beautiful adventure.

But he wasn't one to keep off either. 'Stay warned,' he said. 'He is good with women. In fact, women melt like wax in his arms.'

Mira turned. Her face had gone shades of grey. Women melt like wax? Was she melting like wax? Over a cup of coffee one evening, which meant nothing for anyone? Of course she was. She let out a long breath.

'I know, Rishi,' she said softly. 'I can feel the impact he has had on me after just one brief meeting. Must be happening to everyone he meets. I am not the first one, nor will I be the last. But you know what? This attention, his efforts to make me feel nice, are exciting. So I am just enjoying it. I won't indulge more, I promise.'

Rishi was stumped. His sister didn't speak like this. What had changed overnight? 'Why do you say that?' he asked. 'Do you have any idea what a fantastic woman you are? You underplay yourself.'

She shocked him again. 'Maybe. But I am not the kind of woman who can touch hearts. I don't have a voice—I can't say the right things. I can fit in anywhere, but I am never special.'

The brother rushed towards her. 'What the hell did he tell

you yesterday?' he asked, his voice suddenly loud and rough, his jaws tight.

'He didn't say anything to depress me, Rishi,' Mira assured him. 'Maybe I am a little awestruck, judging myself by the standards of achievers. I am so very proud of you. He said his team in office adores you.' She tried to smile.

Rishi dismissed it. 'Hush, Mira... The family might disown you if you tell them I am talented. No one wants me to be talented. They want me to be obedient and mechanical.' He shot back sarcastically, only to be taken aback once again by what Mira said next.

'Would they? You really think so?' She looked at Rishi. 'Do you remember those photographs dad shot and showed us back at home? Wherever his duty took him, he shot the lifestyles and portraits of those locales. The small thatched-roof shops, the women filling water, snow on pine trees, the sun setting behind a Muslim man reading namaz, a little girl studying, an old man smoking—and there were so many more. Many of those photographs are printed and framed in his study. The only hobby I have known him to pursue is collecting cameras. He has some antique ones, centuries old, and many ultra-modern ones as well, all displayed in the room right at the back of the bungalow in Shimla. He has written out the history of each camera himself on the cases holding them. Only the family members and some of his closest friends are allowed to enter that room.'

She paused, her words soaked in the warmth of fond memories. The brother sat beside her, speechless.

'Had we been together, I think dad would have understood you. You may have inherited a little of this from him. He would have supported you, Rishi. Who knows? He would have been happy that his nephew is doing what he couldn't. He would have been very proud of you.'

Mira's eyes were brimming with tears. She wiped them with the back of her hand. 'So foolishly we have stayed away, Rishi. Everyone has suffered. Can't this end, for heaven's sake?' She sounded agitated.

Her cousin fetched her a glass of water. No one spoke for a long time. Quietly they sat together, thinking about their parents and the house on Raj Bhawan Road. When she had calmed down, Rishi said, 'Browny, I have a plan for the summer.' His eyes were uncertain, but bright. 'We will have to take a risk.'

Mira looked at him in anticipation.

'Let's tell our parents that there is an inter-college, inter-discipline student exchange programme planned out in Mumbai. It's a community-building exercise, in which all students will have to spend fifteen days at another student's house. This is supposed to enhance feelings of fellowship, where they share and care about each other's relations and resources; also, the exercise is aimed at helping them experience an environment different from the one they are used to. This will help students adapt better in life. This summer, I will go to your house and you will go to mine. They won't know who we are. But we will try to say things and make them face situations that remind them of the past. We will make them miss their sibling. We will try to convince them that life is miserable unless we are together.'

Mira's eyes sparkled. 'That is amazing! Sounds great! But what if we get caught?'

'Good for us,' Rishi smiled. 'We'll just cry our hearts out and tell them that we missed them. Not that they aren't missing us too. They just won't confess unless they are provoked enough. Let's try this?'

Mira smiled. The usual innocent smile was back. Summer holidays would be interesting this year!

17.

It was Mira who made the first call.

The heavy-voiced 'Hello' that floated in from the other end of the loudspeaker sent Rishi into splits. Mira glared at him. He covered his mouth and fled, only to reappear in a while to listen in on the conversation.

'Why?' the grim voice of Major General Dhillon asked. 'Should I talk to your college authorities?'

'Who would you talk to? It came as a circular. It is a programme designed by a few colleges together. It doesn't mention one person or group that initiated this.' Mira sounded tense.

Rishi whispered from behind, shaking his fist. 'Confidence, Browny, confidence. Don't panic.'

She took a deep breath. 'Moreover, I have volunteered for this. It was not compulsory,' she said with resolve.

'What!' the father screamed, making Rishi cover his mouth and run again. 'Why did you volunteer?'

Mira turned towards the window so she could avoid the stupid reactions of her brother. 'Dad, it is a beautiful initiative, where students get to live each other's lives. We always think that the other side of the grass is greener. We judge people that way. But what about stepping into someone else's shoes and experiencing things some other way? There might be so much to learn for all of us here.'

Her father still didn't buy the argument. 'What nonsense! I have given my life to the Army. Now someone else will show me how to live life?'

'So many times our happiness is controlled by the insensitivity of others, Dad. Who knows, maybe the opposite also works? We just need to give them a chance.' Mira's voice was heavy with tears and nostalgia. This silenced the Major. When she didn't get a response, Mira spoke again, very softly this time. 'Only two weeks, Dad. Please, let's try this out.'

Finally, her father said, 'I haven't known you to be smart enough to be able to live with complete strangers in a new city.'

'Trust me, Dad, all security checks have been done by the colleges already. So it is absolutely safe,' Mira lied.

'I don't trust your college. Let me know where you are. I will get my network to check it out.' He paused. 'See you after those two weeks. I hope there won't be any more voluntary programmes after this.'

The phone went dead. Rishi raised both his hands in the air.

Mira turned towards him. 'That was pretty easy,' she quipped. And then, with eyebrows raised, she asked, 'Why were you giggling?'

Rishi imitated his uncle, copying the signature intonations. Mira fell on the bed laughing.

'He is still such a Mogambo,' he said.

The sister was quick to remind him, 'It's your turn now.'

Rishi nodded. 'Let's do this at night.' He looked around for his bag.

'Why not now?' Mira insisted.

Rishi didn't answer. She asked again. He spoke, a little

bitterly, 'Because if I speak to mom now, I'll have to bear the burden of whatever I hear from her for the rest of the day. At night I will just have a word with her and fall sleep.' Ending the conversation abruptly, he rushed to take a bath.

One hour later, Rishi walked unmindfully through his college compound. The colourfully painted walls of IAD seemed to assure him that everything would be fine. Convincing his uncle was no big deal. Mira had always been a good child, obedient and uncomplicated. Her father knew she was not capable of doing anything that could shock her humble understanding of life. He was a man of few words anyway, unwilling to carry on a conversation for too long. He thought about his uncle and smiled. The man must be sitting now with a deep trench between his eyebrows, with Saundarya Ma wailing beside him that the girl had already started taking chances and that it wasn't a good sign. After having heard enough of her laments and thinking about the issue at hand from all aspects, he would call Akshat Uncle and request him to visit Mira.

Simple and predictable. Like Mira.

Akshat Uncle was a family friend. He was Rishi's mother's classmate, and had joined the Army three years after his uncle. When Mira had come to Mumbai, he had called. Soon after, the three of them had met at Gulmohar Café inside IIT Bombay and the two cousins had made him privy to their little secret—that Rishi and Mira were living in the same flat. Obviously, he didn't say a word to the Major or his sister. The rift between the siblings had been as much of a shock to him as it had been to their own families.

Rishi didn't need to be told that they were meeting Akshat Uncle sometime soon. He would once again go back with a secret. He nodded. Mira's part of the plan was sorted.

But Rishi's wasn't.

There would be endless speculations and questions. There would be insinuations that he was forcing his personal whims on his family once again. Once again, he would be reminded that he had brought shame to his professor parents with a career choice that would lead nowhere.

He closed his eyes and covered his face with both hands. He waited for a few seconds to get a grip on himself before entering class. His eyes searched for a quiet corner; they stumbled on another obstacle instead. The girl three benches away was passing glances at him. He smiled back in a desperate attempt to distract himself. She smiled back, a little too much.

'Isn't it your birthday today?' he asked, vaguely remembering a Facebook update.

'How do you know?' The girl was shocked. He shrugged and wished her. The rest of the class followed. Even the professor spent two of his precious minutes to congratulate her on one more useless year on earth.

'What was that?' Poncho asked, as they walked out of class. When he didn't get an answer, he pushed his unusually unmindful friend.

'What! Oh that? A Facebook update,' he said nonchalantly.

'How do you do this, man?' Poncho shook his head, looking sad.

Rishi pointed at his belly. 'Shed this. Be fit. You will feel better and everything else will follow.'

'But how?'

'Come, let's try it out now.' Ignoring Poncho's violent protests, he dragged the poor boy towards the field, where some students were playing football.

A few hours later, the college common board found a perfectly sketched caricature of the professor in class. Its mysterious creator left no signature; neither were the authorities in a hurry to nab the culprit. Though the concerned professor expressed neither approval nor anger, the teacher's room was loud and cheerful, debating the sketch and laughing about the professor's 'slip' moments captured with fantastic precision.

That evening, when Rishi came home, Mira was waiting for him. All day he had tried to keep his mind off the task at hand. Now he had no choice but to face it. He took a bath, munched on a bun and sat down beside her.

He dialled the home's landline number. No one picked up. After twenty minutes he called again. This time, it was answered.

'Sharat Bahl here,' his father's voice came from the other end. Mira drew closer, eager to hear the long-lost voices again. Rishi was happy that his mom hadn't taken the call. It was always easier with dad.

'Actually, dad…' he started. He was cut short.

'We know about your community programme bullshit. Akshat had called up this evening to tell us. Don't people in Mumbai have any work other than messing up others' lives?'

'You know?' Rishi asked, shocked, and looked at a smiling Mira.

'Deepti, obviously, is not happy. But Akshat convinced her that this was a noble initiative and that all security checks had been done. Why did you have to volunteer?'

'Dad...' Rishi tried to speak again, but Sharat Bahl wasn't listening.

'You do all kinds of strange things and I have to hear about it for months after. Can't you just be like any other normal boy? When will you act a little maturely? And if you aren't ready to act mature, then take your mom along. Why should I face the music for someone else's strange habits?'

Rishi smiled. 'Why don't you come here and stay with me, Dad? I miss you...' he added dramatically, and Mira slapped him from behind.

'Shut up! Idiot,' his father cut him off.

'Where's mom?' Rishi asked.

'Gone out shopping. She feels that the curtains are too old and bed sheets too worn for anyone new coming to stay with us. So a new look for the house is on the cards. You know how this lady tries to find excuses for shopping... She left in the evening—there has been no sign that she's coming back any time soon. She spends money as if she is Amitabh Bachchan's wife,' his father complained.

Rishi was laughing now. 'Who Amitabh Bachchan? You are the baap of all Bachchans.'

'Cut the crap,' Sharat Bahl said. 'On second thoughts, I think I am happy that a stranger is coming to stay with us. At least the house will be peaceful for a while. Deepti will be better-behaved.'

The son fell silent. The father spoke again. 'Just do me a favour and get yourself some brain detox before you come, so you have more to do here than fight with your mom. Else I will spray chloroform on both of you.' He hung up.

After this unexpectedly animated conversation with his father, Rishi felt like a huge load had been lifted off his shoulders. He looked at Mira in gratitude.

'What did you tell Akshat Uncle?'

'I called and told him about our plan. He was very encouraging and wanted to help.'

'Then?' Rishi probed.

'I told him that you were too scared to talk to Deepti Bua. So it would be nice if he could convince her.' She chuckled. Rishi frowned.

'I am not scared of mom! Just that...' He turned and found Mira laughing.

He chased her; she ran.

18.

'Who goes for a three-week summer holiday during M.Tech?' Professor Shayan Chatterjee didn't ask her, but his eyes said it all. She confirmed that by the time she'd return, she'd be done with writing the theory for her thesis. Summer holidays were about to begin and the usual buzz in the campus was gone. Leisurely Mira walked up to Kunj Bihari's stall. He seemed tense.

'That man was here again yesterday, Mira Didi. He's dangerous,' he said, voice lowered to a husky whisper.

'Which man?' Mira frowned.

'The one who always tries to act smart. I saw him walking with two of the professors here. Stay away from him, Mira Didi. I think he practises black magic. Don't think those designs on his body are harmless.'

Strange! Viyaan had been here! Her mood immediately changed. Why hadn't he told her? But then, why would he? A coincidental meeting that led to a coffee one evening didn't mean it had to become a regular activity. So what if he had gifted her a little teddy and made a cartoon for her? She bid farewell to Kunj Bihari for the summer and promised to stay away from Tattoo Man.

On her way back, she shopped—a sari for Deepti Bua and a shirt for Sharat Uncle. She picked up some snacks for the way and headed home. Rishi was playing some strange hip hop music on his laptop in full volume. The entire room was a mess. The wardrobe was open, clothes scattered all around and empty bottles of body spray lay on the bed. He sat among all of this, munching on wafers.

Mira gave him a hard punch and started packing his luggage. He sat near the window, giving her regular instructions. At 5 p.m., they headed to the station. Mira's train was at 7.15 and Rishi's at 9.35. She boarded the train and looked at her brother.

'What will you do for two hours?'

'I will miss my Kohli.' He made a face.

Soon the train hooted. From the closed glass window, she looked at her brother on the platform. Tension seeped through her. What if they recognized her? She drank some water and pulled out her diary.

Problem No. 3,305: Sita Sharma! That was to be her temporary name in Bengaluru.

Early next morning, Mira pulled her luggage out on the Bengaluru station. The last time she had travelled to a new city, Rishi was there to help. This time she didn't feel like hiring a porter. At the centre of her suitcase was written 'Major General A.K. Dhillon'. Rishi had sprayed some colour over it to cover the name. Now the suitcase looked as if it belonged to a hippie. She ran her fingers over the painted-over name. As the cab drove her to Cooke's Town, she wiped the sweat off her forehead.

'What if...?' she dared not think. This had to work.

The cab stopped in front of Block D of Yashodhara Society. Mira paid the driver and looked around. Beautiful gardens, pebbled paths lined with vibrant shrubs, and three floors of parking. Some late-risers in shorts and ganjees walked briskly past, sweating profusely in the sun. The clubhouse was built in the middle of the society. 'Club, auditorium, swimming pool, gym, squash and tennis,' said a board hung on the wall of the clubhouse. The Bahls had shifted here some twelve years back, when Sharat Bahl had joined Bangalore University as a professor of English Literature. His wife had been planning to shift to a new city for a long time. The arrangement seemed perfect. She had settled down as a professor of Physics at Christ University. Mira had just pulled out her mobile to send a text to Rishi when a voice from behind her made her turn.

Short and thin, with red eyes, he spoke a lot. The watchman. She didn't understand a word. He explained again, this time with a deep frown; signs of displeasure showed on his face. Having stayed with Saundarya all these years, she had learnt a few Tamil words. She attempted to apply them all. They messed things up far more than they sorted out!

'Should I call up Bua and ask her to come downstairs?' she thought, but changed her mind immediately. 'No, I can't disturb her unnecessarily.'

She tried to explain in English, then in Hindi. But the frowns just got deeper. This time the watchman called another guard from the main gate of the society. They checked the register where the cab driver had made an entry.

'703?' The red eyes looked at her.

Mira nodded vigorously.

'Sharat Bahl?'

She nodded again.

This time he seemed to smile, very faintly. He picked up her luggage and walked briskly towards the lift, with Mira trying to keep up to make sure he didn't disappear with her bags. It was the watchman who rang the bell at 703. Mira stood behind him, praying that the introduction would go well. The door opened.

Deepti Bua looked older than her years. White hair sneaked out, despite her attempts to colour them black. She had put on weight. With puffy eyes and a strict face, she stood at the door, eyes fixed on Mira. She inspected her for a few seconds and turned to dismiss the over-enthusiastic watchman. Mira tried to give him a tip; she gestured her not to. Carefully, she walked past the short guy to enter the flat. She wanted to hug her aunt; she ended up touching her feet instead.

The elderly lady gave her a faint smile and asked her to sit. She went inside. Mira looked around. On the wall at the far end, Rishi's photographs were displayed. Right from when he was a newborn to his recent ones. Each frame captured a happy moment that belied his present conflicts with his parents. Her father wasn't in any of the photographs. But she identified the one on the left—it had been clicked by him. She was staring at it when someone loudly cleared his throat from behind. She turned.

'Usually it's my wife who stands there staring at that photograph. I had just started to rejoice that she had suddenly grown young. Tough luck.' A warm smile lit up his face.

Mira smiled back. Sharat Uncle had always been a man of great humour. Other than his glasses and a few loose stretches on his skin, he looked almost the same. His next sentence sent a cold wave down her spine.

'Have we met before?' He seemed to be racking his memory to place her. She walked up to him, touched his feet and then stood a few steps away. Sharat Uncle was still inspecting her keenly.

'No, Sir, we haven't,' she said softly. Deepti Bua's shrill voice relieved the anxiety that threatened to grip Mira, interrupting the elderly man's chain of thought.

'He feels everyone he meets is his student. You can trust English professors to be desperate,' Deepti Bua had a tray on which stood three glasses of cola. There was latent humour in the comment, but she did not smile. Sharat Uncle raised an eyebrow. 'She is an M.Tech student, Deepti. You perhaps did not recognize her because she is far from being the rare experiment of radioactive rays, like you.' He laughed aloud without waiting for anyone to react.

Before Deepti Bua could give him a comeback, Mira changed the topic. 'Is that your son?'

Deepti Bua nodded. Sharat Uncle laughed again. 'No, darling. He is the neighbour's fantasy. These photographs they dumped on us because the lady of the house collects antique pieces. The lad you see displayed there is as much a rare treasure as she is.'

Deepti Bua turned red, but chose to ignore her husband. Mira pinched herself to stop herself from laughing.

'You are an engineering student. Very nice. Science gives you logic and rationalism. You don't end up saying anything and everything that comes to your mind, unlike other people.' She looked at the 'other people' on her right, and then back at

Mira. Mira stole a glance at both of them. The main challenge of staying in this house, she realized, would be to check her laughter every time these two took a dig at each other.

'So where are you from? What do your parents do?' Deepti Bua asked.

'I am from Delhi. My mother is no more. My father owns a chain of sari shops. There's one in Karol Bagh, one in Kalkaji and two in South Extension.'

She could see both the faces in front losing their enthusiasm. A sari-shop owner from Delhi didn't excite the professors. Rishi had advised her to say this. 'Any other profession, be it an IT person or an architect or a doctor or an IPS officer, will make them find some common source and want to get in touch with your family. The best way to discourage them is to give them a background they won't connect with,' Rishi had warned her. The idiot had suggested that she say her father was the owner of grocery stores. After much argument, she had agreed to be the daughter of a businessman dealing in zardosi and chikan saris.

She looked at the grim faces staring at her. She tried not to think of her father, and what he would think of suddenly being turned into a sari-shop owner.

Sharat Uncle was the first to break the silence and change the topic. 'Here in Bengaluru everyone has this habit of adding an extra "h" to the names. So I am "Sharath" and this is "Deepthi". Don't be surprised if you become "Sitha"!' He laughed.

Sitha? Oh, Sita! She had completely forgotten about her fake name. Akshat Uncle had already introduced her as 'Sita' to the couple. He had even got her to suspend her Facebook profile, so Mira Dhillon was sufficiently wiped out from the

Internet. Couldn't she have assumed any other name? Her cousin had explained that a sari shop owner at Kalkaji would be a conservative, ritualistic, UP Brahmin. It made sense for her to assume such a name. Utter nonsense!

She smiled, albeit helplessly.

'In fact,' Sharat Uncle continued, 'pick up the language here if you can. That's the way to make friends fast…' But Deepti Bua cut him short.

'She's here only for fifteen days. Let her just look around and enjoy.' She smiled at Mira. 'Your uncle is an encyclopaedia of languages. He speaks quite a few Indian dialects, and Spanish. He wants everyone around him to follow suit. When you know too many languages, you find it difficult to express yourself appropriately. You blabber more than you talk. When data codes travel through multiple sources, they lose their sharpness. Simple science of communication. Here.'

She held out a plate of cookies towards her. Those were Deepti Bua's special home-made cookies. The aroma brought back a thousand memories. She lifted one and looked at Sharat Uncle, perhaps to see if he expected her to reject the offering in protest of his wife's insulting digs.

'Please eat.' He smiled mischievously. 'In this house, only her rants will challenge your metabolism. The rest are safe.'

They got up soon and Deepti Bua led her inside. The room she opened for her was huge, with a large balcony, yellow walls and beautiful paintings.

'This is my son's room,' she said. 'The air conditioner isn't working in the guest room. You might as well use this one.' She turned to find Mira looking at one of the oil paintings on the wall. It showed a large flower-laden gulmohar tree. An old, deserted bungalow stood behind it, with broken windows and an unkempt terrace. Silently, the older woman turned to leave.

'Ma'am,' Mira called from behind. 'It's beautiful. It looks so real.'

Deepti Bua looked at it and left without a word. Mira wasn't surprised. The corner of the painting had her brother's signature. She didn't need to be told that the painting was a reflection of their ancestral house. The gulmohar tree still stood there, but the house had been abandoned by the family in Bengaluru.

Mira unpacked and prepared to go for a bath. But then she sat down on the floor and fished out her mobile phone from her handbag. It had three missed calls already. She dialled back.

'Are you nuts, Browny? Can't you just inform me that you've reached?' The voice yelled from the other end. Mira knew how to put that back in place.

'I am staying in your room.' She chuckled.

'Why?' Rishi asked immediately. 'What happened to the guest room?'

'Call and ask,' she mocked.

'Okay, listen carefully,' Rishi began, 'don't try to arrange my drawers and cupboards. You have this nasty habit of packing off my stuff neatly. Then I can never get what I want. Just stay away. I locate my things better when they are messed up. Clear?'

'I won't have to do that. I guess Deepti Bua has done that already.' She laughed, leaving her cousin even more irritated.

'How is it going? Enjoying the circus?' he finally asked.

'They are still so much the same,' Mira sighed. 'They still fight like college friends trying to outwit each other.'

'Friends?' Rishi seemed shocked. 'They were never friends. They represented two opposition parties in their college union.

Mom still holds the fact that dad got more votes than her against him. Friends, my foot! God knows who got them married, and how!'

'You've reached?' Mira asked. 'How's the scene there?'

'Not yet.' The brother giggled. 'I am in Gurgaon. Will get there tomorrow.'

Mira grew anxious. 'Dad will be waiting for you. What do you mean you'll reach tomorrow?'

'Let him wait. Don't worry, Browny, I'll handle it.'

'What important work is waiting for you in Gurgaon?' she asked sarcastically. In her mind she could see her restless father pacing up and down the portico, waiting for his guest to arrive. He didn't like people who weren't punctual. But Rishi was one stubborn boy who would never reveal what was going on in his mind. He was deliberately trying to irk his uncle, she had no idea why.

He disconnected the phone.

Late that evening, before Mira put her phone on charge, she checked for WhatsApp messages. Rishi had sent a few images. They seemed to be of a huge bungalow, beautifully done up in geometric blocks. The idiot stood before it with a placard that read 'Virat Kohli's house'. Shocked, she checked for more photographs. In front of the same house, the lunatic had posed with a cake designed like a cricket field, that read 'Kohli's Fanboy'. There was a video of him and two other boys cutting the cake and raising a toast to the cricketer.

Mira went back to the call log to warn her brother that he had to run before Kohli got him arrested, but the phone was already beeping with a call from another number.

Her father's!

19.

Akshat Uncle had called Rishi to inform him that the moustache was dialling every number on his mobile phone to locate the 'boy'!

'These military people don't have any patience,' Rishi decided. 'If I am not there on time, just sit with a beer and munch on some nuts, man. This brother-sister duo is just too alike. They love to control others' lives.'

Slowly he opened the gate and entered.

The bus had dropped him at the Victory Tunnel stop on Cart Road. Memories had rushed in the moment he had set foot in Shimla. Instead of taking a cab, he had walked the distance. The taxi drivers scouting for passengers did not appreciate such tourists. They followed him, expecting that sooner or later he would get tired and hire one of them. Every other minute they asked whether he had changed his mind. Eventually they muttered abuses and left.

He walked at his leisure, stopping wherever he wanted to, asking the people around what had happened to a small shop here or a little hut there or a temple that had stood at the corner of the street sixteen years ago. Too many hotels had come up around the place; and there were too many people. It had rained that morning. The weather was foggy and the road slippery. The cool breeze of Shimla cut into his skin. He hugged himself tight but kept walking.

The Raj Bhawan Road house stood exactly as it used to. Calm—almost depressing—till he ran inside and got everyone on their feet. That he would, in a few seconds. He chose to walk over the grassy lawn, instead of taking the pebbled path. When he was a child, this used to irritate his mother. She would shout at him for getting mud on his shoes from the wet grass. He was halfway across when a watchman came running.

'Hey!' he shouted. 'Get back on the path. Right now.'

Amused, he obeyed. He was guided towards the main door of the house. They entered the hall and walked towards the living area. Rishi glanced to the left, at the room from where Nani's affectionate voice would call out to him every time he entered, 'I can smell an angel prince in this house. I can feel music in the air; there is so much brightness all around.' The feeble yet melodious voice would wait for Rishi to run to her and hug her. She never screamed at him for touching her before he had washed up. The old lady only hugged him back and blessed him. Her words echoed in his mind and his steps slowed down. They had come to know of her demise from Akshat Uncle. His mother had wept for days. 'Let's go there, Deepti,' his dad had suggested. But she hadn't relented.

'What happened?' the watchman asked, suspiciously looking at the boy now staring at the empty room on the left.

Rishi shook his head and started walking again. Soon, he was standing before the Major. For the first few seconds, he went completely numb. Uncle and nephew looked at each other, silent. The same athletic build, eyebrows knitted together into a deep frown, an aura of strength emanating from his uncle's personality and the disgruntled look without which he was incomplete. Rishi tried not to laugh. There were some whites visible in his uncle's black hair and moustache, his skin seemed softer than it used to be, but there was the same toughness that characterized every line in his face. It took him a few moments to talk without his emotions getting the better of him.

'*Pranaam, Chacha,*' he ran to the Major and hugged him. The man stiffened from this sudden breach of physical privacy from a stranger. 'I am Rahul Pandey.' He took the Major's hands into his and shook them with great enthusiasm. 'I really like the Army kind of people. They are very macho. I saw Akshay Kumar in this film, *Holiday.* It showed that Army people get no holiday, only duty wherever they go. You must be getting discounts for all the grocery and stuff you buy, no? Lucky, you people. My mother keeps cribbing that the prices are rising alarmingly these days.' He paused, enjoying the expressions on his uncle's face. The man glared at him, as if hoping his gaze would burn the skin off his guest.

'Go and wash up. And wash your shoes as well. You have left muddy prints on the floor. And yes, call me Major, not Chacha,' he said as coldly as he could, and then looked at the watchman. 'Show him his room.'

Rishi gave him a stupid smile and turned to leave, but instead put his arm around the watchman. 'What's your name, brother?' he asked, as they both disappeared.

The Major spotted Saundarya hiding behind a curtain, stealthily observing the boy.

'Didn't I tell you not to let in a random boy coming from nowhere? See what he has done to the floor. God knows what family, which caste, he belongs to! And who talks like that? You get discounts for grocery! Is that all he finds in the life of a Major General? So stupid! You should have slapped him.' The woman didn't even pause for breath as the words tumbled out of her. 'Now wait and watch what a joke people make of your daughter. Very soon my beautiful Mira will speak this language too.' She left the room in a huff, leaving the man to fume on his own.

Upstairs, behind closed doors, Rishi let out the laughter he had been holding in for so long.

'You should have seen him, Browny, when I called him chacha. I am sure he wanted to shoot me.'

'Why do you love to irritate people? What do you get out of it?' Mira laughed too.

Her brother ignored her. 'He and his military perfection. The mud stains, the hug... He almost puked.'

'Don't exaggerate,' the sister reprimanded. 'He has lived in severe conditions and has spent time in dirtier places than you can imagine. Yes, the house is his temple. Did he feel he had seen you somewhere before?'

'No,' Rishi assured her. 'I distracted him too much with my "obnoxious" behaviour right from the start.' He laughed again.

Mira shrugged. 'Sharat Uncle said he found me familiar.' This made her cousin sit up.

'Careful, Browny. My dad is sharper than my mom gives him credit for.'

At the same time, downstairs, Major General Dhillon was talking to his friend, Major Akshat Tiwari.

'Can you believe this? He came wearing a stupid pair of knee-length pants.'

'You expected him to wear a tie and a blazer while travelling by train?' his friend asked.

'Come on, Akshat. I was in my formals, waiting to welcome him. A shirt, trousers and a good pair of shoes don't harm. What you wear and how you appear in front of people show your respect for them. And then there was his worn-out backpack. He had a silly shirt tied across his dirty bag to hold the water bottle in the torn side pocket in place. This is ridiculous!' he blurted out, as his friend laughed from the other end. 'I tried to call up Mira. She is busy talking to someone over the phone.'

'What would you tell Mira? She isn't responsible for the boy who has reached your door. These are external decisions,' his friend said.

'I am worried about her, Akshat,' the Major admitted.

'Don't be,' his friend assured him. 'I have checked on Mira myself. She is in good company. She will tell you more when she calls you back.'

Akshat Tiwari could hear a deep sigh from the other end. He smiled. 'The boy is a genius, Anil. Try not to judge him by his antics. When I met him, he reminded me of you. The Anil I knew some forty years back. The one who used to disappear into the woods to photograph a whistling bird. Kids of each new generation follow the norms of their times. Accept that, and you are good.'

'Mira isn't like that,' the father argued back.

'And where does that land her?' his friend asked directly. 'She is unique and beautiful, but she struggles in a crowd. She finds it difficult to make friends, she can't speak firmly, she stays closed in her little space expecting someone to find her.' Akshat Tiwari paused. 'Now that she is getting the exposure she deserves, just let her be. It's good for her.'

They disconnected. From the window the Major could see

the boy. Wearing a T-shirt and pyjamas now, freshly bathed, he didn't look as bad. Almost decent. A camera hung around his neck, he was roaming around the lawn, as if looking for something. The Major came outside and stood on the veranda. He came downstairs to the garden, walking towards the boy.

It had been so long that Rishi had stood in that garden. He felt like a child again, chasing fluttering butterflies. Rishi aimed his camera at some; they flew away. He grunted in frustration. The Major stood a little distance away from the flower beds, watching him. The boy spotted him and walked towards him, smiling.

'Beautiful garden. Beautiful flowers,' the boy said, as he checked his camera. The Major was tempted to see what he had captured in his DSLR, but stopped himself. Sunny approached him with a cup of coffee. But before the Major could pick up his cup from the tray, the boy grabbed it and took a sip, not bothering to even look at either of them. Sunny was about to give the boy a piece of his mind, but a look from his employer silenced him. He headed back to the kitchen to get another cup, muttering profanities.

'I wish there were marigolds here. You guys don't like marigolds?' Rishi asked with a deep frown.

The corner of the garden that used to be his dream spot was now full of yellow, purple and maroon flowers. Those big, round marigolds in stunning shades of yellow and orange were nowhere to be seen. He remembered how Shiraz used to take freshly plucked marigolds to Nani's room in a cane basket for her morning puja. Amid smells of camphor and incense sticks, she would close her eyes and fold her hands, asking a world of favours from the Almighty. God had taken away her only daughter, but He couldn't take away her unrelenting faith in His goodness.

Before venturing out into the garden, Rishi had visited her room. It was still very much the same. Just that the old woman on the bed had been reduced to a photograph on the wall. The room didn't have the familiar, comforting smell of her body any more, just some cold, impersonal artefacts.

The Major's voice jolted him out of his reverie.

'We had a bed of beautiful marigolds once. They went away with the gardener.' He let out a breath, turned and walked away.

What does that mean? Gardener... Shiraz? Where did he go? Rishi ran inside and looked around for Saundarya.

'What did you tell him now? Why is he upset?' the woman asked curtly, without caring for any formal introduction.

'You talk like my mother,' Rishi smiled. Her hands, busy arranging a pile of clothes, stopped. 'What do I call you?'

'Call me Aunty,' she said shortly.

'I just said that the garden would look better if it had a bed of marigolds. That can't be offensive, can it?' Rishi couldn't bring himself to play the pranks he usually did with the others. Something about Saundarya Ma made him sober. Her deft hands slowed down; a few of the hangers she was folding the clothes neatly on to slipped. There were tears in her eyes. She wiped them with a corner of her sari. 'A misfortune befell this house. A curse. A bad omen,' she sniffed.

'What are you talking about?' Rishi was growing impatient.

'We had a man who had been tending the garden for years. Shiraz.' The lady said softly. 'He grew beautiful marigolds. He was very fond of them. And maybe the flowers understood his devotion. So many times I have seen him talking to them. They almost spoke back to him. He knew which plant would grow how tall and what exact shade the flowers would be.'

Rishi smiled. He, too, remembered Shiraz talking to the plants.

'He died of a snakebite some six years back. He didn't notice a snake lurking behind his favourite flowers... After him, the garden was no longer the same. The marigolds died. A new gardener came and tried to salvage the plants, but nothing worked. He uprooted them all and tried to build the bed again. The stems shot up, the leaves appeared. But they rotted just before the flowers came. Shiraz's death has left a curse on the soil. It took away the marigolds forever.'

She turned to look at Rishi. She was surprised to see the look on his face. He seemed shocked, devastated.

'What happened?' Saundarya was concerned. 'Are you fine? You need water?' But Rishi wasn't listening.

Shiraz was no more! Shiraz, the magician from his childhood, their 'fairy-tale man'. When bonfires were lit and the flames touched the skies, he would sit in a corner and tell them stories. Kings' horses whose manes would flow as spectacularly as the fire. Giants. Princesses. Castles. Jewels. And marigolds, which had the power to bring the dead back to life. Marigolds played a significant, life-altering role in all his stories. That Shiraz was no more? Couldn't he just touch the flowers and get back his life? Couldn't the flowers help him come back, like he described in his stories?

'Why didn't anyone rush him to the hospital?' he asked softly. 'Poison takes time to spread.'

A little confused by the reactions of the boy, Saundarya nodded sadly. 'Shiraz entered the garden even before the sun was up. Like all other days, we were asleep when he came. At 8 in the morning, Sunny went to the garden to serve him his cup of tea. He found him lying there, lifeless.' She paused. 'God knows when the snake had entered. It could have been any of us. Shiraz took the death upon himself. But before he died, he killed the snake. We saw a dagger by his side and the limp body of the snake next to it. We owe Shiraz our lives; there is no way we can pay back his debt.' She wiped her tears.

'So many people have left us, those who meant the world to this house. They never looked back. Didn't even think twice before leaving us behind. And the poor Major. He never utters a word, never sheds a tear. He just carries that grief around in his heart.'

Rishi had grown silent too. She looked at his ashen face. 'Did you know Shiraz?'

The boy shook his head. 'No.' He got up and left, leaving the old woman bewildered.

20.

She missed Rishi.

Whenever he was around, Mira was a ball of energy. Without him life became so quiet. She felt sad. Her days had never been as happening as they were in Mumbai. She had never laughed so much, never spent so much time outside, as she had in the last few months.

Mira stood on the balcony, watching people walk briskly on the joggers' path below. From the other end of the house, the voices of Deepti Bua and Sharat Uncle taking potshots at each other reached her.

'You drank my tea?'

'I found it on the table, I thought it was for me.'

'Ridiculous, Sharat. Why do you and your son have this irritating habit of taking the easy route? You should have asked me.'

'Because you and your son are masters in lecturing. Early in the morning I wanted to save my brain the stress, which, of course, seems possible no more.'

'I don't understand how your students deal with you. Do you just go and teach them whatever book you find lying on the table? Or you do care to look at the syllabus? Your students must be laughing at you.'

'Oh, come on, Deepti. My students love me! Literature is

not Physics, that I have to compulsively follow a syllabus. I can fly around, like a bird, comparing ideals across ages and continents. But you poor thing, you have to stick to a few rigid books and their funny laws. The only thing that flows in Physics is liquid! How worthless is that?' He laughed. 'And don't make me open my mouth about students. Remember how you wept when we were newly married and you found a love letter in my bag? You made it hell for me, Deepti.'

'Shut up!' Deepti Bua whispered. 'There's a girl staying with us. You have no common sense. Just open your mouth and blurt out anything that comes to mind.'

Mira smiled, standing on the balcony, behaving like she couldn't hear a word.

'Your students are scared of you. Mine love me. Don't change the topic.' Sharat Uncle continued to tease her. Deepti Bua fumed. But she said something which immediately got Mira to prick up her ears.

'Did he call?' she asked.

'He is having a ball of a time in Chandigarh.'

Deepti Bua sighed. 'God knows what will happen to this boy.'

'Maybe we are thinking too much. Come on, Deepti, he's our son. He is as stubborn as you and as romantic as me. Yes, I know, as hopelessly romantic as me.' Sharat Uncle stopped her as Deepti Bua prepared to come back with a repartee. 'Accept it, Deepti. He has made a choice.'

'Accept what, Sharat?' His wife sounded upset. 'He might think he is creating masterpieces, but tomorrow they may not sell. As good as he might be with his art, people may not like it. Then what? Where will he go? What will he eat? His stupid dreams? At least have an academic degree to fall back on, so that you have other avenues to earn from!'

'Deepti, his photographs got accepted by the National Geographic...' Sharat Uncle said softly.

Deepti Bua frowned. 'Where on earth do you think up such lame support from? Today anyone can submit their photographs with Nat Geo and get them published. What's the big deal?' She took a deep breath. 'All I wanted him to do was complete his graduation. But that, too, hurt his ego. What kind of person drops out after reaching their final year in B.A.? What degree will this arts course fetch him? Where will he go in life with such high-headedness? Who does he think cares for this nonsense?'

Mira was getting increasingly uncomfortable. She tried to concentrate on the vegetable vendors standing around lazily with their wares at one end of the society. It was too early for anyone to come out vegetable-shopping on a Saturday. Car cleaners splashed the parked cars with water and chatted among themselves. The watchman came and said something to them, perhaps to keep it low, and they stopped, only to start again in a few seconds.

Mira sighed and was startled to find Sharat Uncle standing right behind her.

'What do you think about so much?' he asked with a smile, as he handed her a cup of tea. 'You want to come down with me for a walk?'

Mira nodded. Soon they were downstairs, revelling in the morning sun and walking as a gentle breeze blew. A few other gentlemen from the society joined them. They spoke among themselves, shared jokes, discussed cricket and argued for and against PM Modi, panted with the energy spent, and walked on. When they were tired, they sat down on the benches on the sides of the society garden. One of the gentlemen made a call and, soon, cups of tea for everyone came from his kitchen.

Sharat Uncle specially introduced Mira to him. 'Everyone in Bengaluru knows about Murthy's taste for beverages. He is a complete beverage freak. His house is a temple of different flavours of tea, sourced from countries around the world. In fact, he is now setting up his own tea boutique. It is supposed to be a one-of-its-kind café in Asia. He's using up all the money he has earned his entire life to fulfil this dream. He's rich, smart—and brave.'

Mira smiled at Sanjay Murthy. He invited them to his café with his heavily accented South Indian English. 'The interiors are being done. Why don't you guys drop in sometime? We want every inch of the café to celebrate the spirit of Bengaluru. Come and give me your feedback.'

It was decided they would pay his store a visit that evening. As they walked back, Mira looked at Sharat Uncle. 'Why did you call him rich, smart and brave?'

'In a few days he will see his dream come to life. He will be able to touch it. Can anyone be richer than that?'

'You know the painting that hangs on the wall of the room I sleep in—that, too, is a dream. The artist is rich,' she said softly, hoping she'd not offend the father. Sharat Uncle stiffened. 'I am sorry, I couldn't help overhearing your conversation in the morning,' Mira confessed. She prayed that he wouldn't tell her it was none of her business. He didn't.

'That's fine. We were not being discreet either.' He tried to appear comfortable. Mira tried to help. 'When parents refuse to understand us, it hurts.'

'We're not sure our son knows what he's doing.' Sharat Uncle looked sad. 'He has always been a maverick. His priority is to enjoy life. Actually, he prioritizes himself over life. Indulgence is good, but, for security, you need a Plan B. He doesn't have one. For him, it always has to be the way he wants, and nothing else.'

What Mira said next took the professor by surprise.

'I resist, what is not to be
I perish, if I am not me.'

She smiled as the professor looked at her, bewildered. 'I found this written in a dairy in your library. Guess it was your handwriting.'

Sharat Uncle looked away.

'Is poetry only a jugglery of words? A philosophy? A preaching that does not need to be practised?'

Sharat Uncle pulled out a cigarette from his pocket and lit it. He took a puff, sending uncertain rings of smoke in the air. After a suffocatingly long silence, he spoke again.

'Poems were my love once upon a time. My wife fell for me over those. Then she wasn't the Physics professor she is today.' He smiled. 'In the humdrum of life, that passion in me disappeared for good. But it was nice of you to read and remember it. But, hey, wait, do you write?'

Mira gave him a shy smile.

'You do? Oh my God. I finally have some company! What the hell are you doing in M.Tech? You must show me what you have written.'

'They aren't good,' she said, suddenly conscious.

'Show it to me, girl. This will be our little secret. Don't tell

Deepti. You are the ideal girl in her perfect physics-dominated world. We should not make that impression suffer.' They both laughed. Unmindfully, he placed a hand on Mira's head, as if blessing her.

*

That evening Sharat Uncle opened the door of the car for Mira. After very long, she had spent time in front of the mirror. A little black bindi and kohl in her eyes did wonders to her face. When she stepped out of the room, Deepti Bua couldn't hold back her surprise.

'Where to?' she asked Sharat Uncle as he stepped into the lift.

'Nowhere special,' he quipped. 'Usually she behaves like a student of engineering, today she is the muse of literature.'

Before Deepti Bua could come up with a reply to that, the door of the lift closed. They both giggled inside.

The car sped towards Koramangala. It stopped in a crowded lane, where Sharat Uncle had to spend a few minutes to find proper parking. Then he guided her towards the back door of a shutters-down shop. On a board was written 'Selvam'. Sharat Uncle explained that it meant 'wealth and beauty' in Tamil. Mira flinched as she walked into the place. It was dirty and dingy. This wasn't meant to be the place for which she had picked out her violet salwar kameez that evening. She had expected a beautiful glass door, which would open out to lavish lights. But Murthy Uncle did say that the place was under construction. Silly of her to assume that the café would look like a five-star restaurant! There were pieces of wood, tattered cloth, ladders and hammers strewn all around. Carpenters were working across the space.

'Come, I will take you to the main sitting area.' Murthy Uncle showed them in. A narrow, dark path led to a half-closed door. It opened into a brightly lit room. This space wasn't dirty, but, rather, unkempt. Two of the walls were covered with cartoons drawn in black ink on a cream base. The drawings showed the beach, markets, coconut trees, temples, offices and sari shops. Funny sketches of people with myriad expressions were thrown in between—some quarrelling with a vendor, some sitting with a laptop, others watching them work, some offering prayers at temples, some selling coconut water and one busy on his mobile phone, while others peeped at the screen over his shoulders. There were many such cute moments captured in the doodles. The walls had acquired a life of their own as the characters narrated stories from the nooks and crannies of a regular day in Bengaluru. Mira didn't know when she had started smiling. She moved forward to take a closer look. She was so engrossed in the doodles that she didn't notice the man sitting above her.

It looked like a ten-foot-long table. The legs of the table were like ladders. The man sat on top of the table, high above the ground, working on the walls.

'Come down, Iyer. We have guests,' Murthy Uncle called out to him.

The harsh voice that came in response shocked Mira.

'Don't you have any patience?' came the irritated reply. Mira frowned. The voice continued. 'Why can't you wait till it is complete? You are killing all the fun by showing it to people in bits and pieces.' A man in dishevelled clothes was climbing down one of the ladder legs.

So rude, Mira thought. She didn't turn to look at the offender. Rather, she concentrated on the cartoons again. This time they didn't seem as cheerful. The gentlemen exchanged introductions and pleasantries, and showered the man with praises. Surprisingly, they didn't seem bothered by his brashness.

'Seems you have offended my young friend here,' Sharat Uncle pointed to Mira. 'Sita, join us.'

'I am willing to apologize endlessly to pretty women.' The man turned and so did Mira—and they both froze.

'Viyaan, this is Sita Sharma,' Murthy Uncle introduced them. 'A guest in the city.'

Confusion replaced the smile on Viyaan's face. Narrowing his eyes, he opened his mouth to say something, but before he could get a word out, Mira rushed towards him, took his left palm in her's and shook it vigorously. 'Hello! I'm Sita. Nice meeting you. Awesome work on the walls!'

The confusion now gave way to a cold stare. The eyes grew serious. A sarcastic nod followed, neither acknowledging nor ignoring her. Viyaan looked back at the two other men.

'I must get back to work. You guys carry on,' he said in a grim tone and climbed back up the ladder swiftly. Mira kept glancing at him till the men said goodbye to each other. Viyaan didn't look at her even once. Mira felt the stress building up near her neck.

Sharat Uncle took her to a beautiful restaurant for refreshments afterwards. Deepti Bua was to join them shortly. Mira felt nervous. She wished she could be alone for a while.

'Can we talk?' she sent a WhatsApp text to Viyaan.

No response.

'Sorry if I offended you.'

Silence from the other end.

'Are you there?'

Her messages went unanswered.

Deepti Bua waved at them as the taxi dropped her near the reception of the restaurant. Mira smiled to confirm she was eager to have her join them. But after a few restless, never-ending minutes of sitting together, she excused herself and went to the restroom. She dialled Rishi's number.

21.

This corner of Shimla used to be so different. An earthen lamp would be lit on the outer wall of the shabby little house. Through the small window, the hustle and bustle of a large family trying to fit into one dark room would be evident. Outside, an earthen stove would be preparing food for the man of the house, his wife, a daughter, a widowed sister, a brother and his wife. In the evening, the wife would put out the fire and spray water on it. Dense smoke would mix with the fog around. Even a stone's throw away, visibility would be poor. Little Rishi would close his eyes and cover his mouth. 'I can't see properly. Why is there so much smoke?'

'That is a magical entrance to destiny, bachcha,' Shiraz would say. 'You see that little door?'

Rishi would blink repeatedly to battle the burning in his eyes, trying to make out the indistinct outlines not too far away. Shiraz would stoop to whisper in his ears.

'Beyond that door, there is happiness. There is truth. There is light. And there is love. There is a fairy who will fulfil all your desires with the touch of her magic wand. But if you have to go there, you will have to overcome this smog. That's the rule of life. This smog will stop you, discourage you; you will be tempted to turn your back and run. But if you can brave it, then the door is yours.'

Shiraz would turn everything into an enchanting story. Today there was no smoke, but Rishi's eyes still watered. He stood near the same rock on which he and Shiraz would often sit, watching the clouds above.

The house was no longer the small, shabby, thatched-roof hut for a crowded family. It was a brick-and-cement structure with three rooms built side by side, and a tap fitted in the courtyard. He stared at it blankly, his mind lost somewhere in images of the past.

'Are you looking for someone, Sir?'

A soft voice cut through the quiet. He turned. A young girl, her head covered with a yellow dupatta and arms holding a pile of crumpled clothes, stood behind him. His silence made her ask again. 'Can I help you?'

'Shabnam?' Rishi asked, an incredulous smile appearing on his face.

The girl frowned and dumped the clothes on a rock. She tried to take a closer look at him, but her face didn't register any recognition. She grew sceptical. 'How do you know my name? And why are you staring at our house?'

'Shiraz used to say there lives a fairy inside this house. Guess I have come looking for her.' He paused as the girl's eyebrows furrowed further. 'I asked him to show me the fairy one day. And he did. A thin, dark girl, hair tied tightly into a pony, snot flowing down her nose, running around barefoot in the house.'

A faint smile seemed to play upon her face now.

'"Is this the fairy?" I had asked, disappointed. And he had laughed loudly. "Look at her through the eyes of a magician," he had said. "You will see a graceful fairy with eyes full of

tenderness, warmth and affection." Shiraz had told me this on
a bright summer morning.'

The girl's resistance had disappeared. She was smiling back
at him now.

'"She is ugly," I had complained. But Shiraz was not angry.
"The ugliness is an illusion, bachcha, a superficial crust… You
have to see through it to reach the real beauty," he had said.'
Rishi looked at the young girl, still thin, but today he could
see a spark in her.

'Who are you, Sir?' She begged that Rishi answer this time.

'Major Dhillon's nephew. You remember me?'

Shabnam's eyes grew large with joy. She opened her mouth,
perhaps to call to those inside her house. But she gasped as
Rishi jumped to cover her mouth with his palm. He gestured
to her to follow him a little further into the eucalyptus forest,
behind one of the bigger trees.

'No one here knows who I am,' he told Shabnam. 'Please
keep it to yourself.' Shabnam was too surprised by the sudden
force to figure out what he was talking about. He explained
in brief, as much as he could—the plan he had hatched with
Mira, how they had landed up at each other's place without
the families knowing who they were.

Shabnam put a finger on her lips. 'Secret,' she promised. 'But
how will I take you inside if I can't tell my mother who you are?'

'You don't have to take me inside.' Rishi leant on the
eucalyptus tree. 'So much has changed, and yet so much hasn't.'
He looked at Shabnam. The afternoon sun had lit up part of
her face. 'What's happening with you guys?' he asked.

A gust of wind caught Shabnam's dupatta and it flew out
of place. She caught hold of the rebellious piece of clothing

and put it back firmly in place.

'After Abbu's death, Major Sahab didn't allow Shabbir Chachu to take up work in the garden. He bought him a taxi instead, so we could earn a better living. Ammi refused to take it, but later agreed when Major Sahab said she could pay back the worth of the vehicle in instalments.'

Shocked, Rishi interrupted. 'Major agreed to take money from you?'

Shabnam smiled. 'He did, but he had something else in mind. Every month whatever money Ammi gives him, he keeps aside for my future. He paid for building this house too; we wouldn't have been able to afford it. Major Sahab was so shaken with Abbu's death, I think he still lives with the guilt,' she said softly.

Rishi looked away.

Shabnam remembered him faintly. He had always been very fair, with sharp features. Everybody loved him because he was cute and naughty. He was the one who forced others to do what he wanted. The only person he obeyed without question was her father. Rishi still had the same effect on people around him. Otherwise, why would she be standing here for so long, waiting to hear more, at the risk of someone catching them in the woods and spreading foul rumours?

They didn't like each other when they were children. Today he was talking like a long-lost friend. He wasn't there to meet her, she knew—Rishi was spending time with the memories of Shiraz. Shabnam glanced at him again. He was staring into nothing. She remembered her father talking about Rishi fondly. 'One day this boy will shine like the sun. Allah will look out for him. The other day, early in the morning, he woke up and called out to me from the balcony. "Shiraaaaaaaaz!" I looked up. Even in the dark, as the moon bade farewell in the western sky, I could see him distinctly. In that fraction of a second, just before I greeted him back, the azan sounded at the mosque. And I knew that this boy was either Allah's favourite, or Allah himself!' Her father's voice rang out in her heart.

'I should get going. It was nice to see you after such a long time,' Rishi said, as he gestured for them to move. But Shabnam stayed put.

'You leave. I will go in a while. I am too close to home; I don't want to be seen coming out of the eucalyptus forest with a young man.' She smiled. Rishi smiled back, embarrassed. Shimla was still a small place. Its people believed whatever they saw. He should have been careful.

'Bye.' He sounded apologetic.

'Bye, Rishi Baba,' Shabnam called from behind, and he stopped.

'Don't call me that. I am Rishi. Only Rishi. But not when anyone is around. The Major and the people at the house know me as Rahul Pandey.'

Surprised, Shabnam asked, 'Who is Rahul Pandey?'

'Well, Rahul is Shah Rukh Khan and Pandey is Salman.' He grinned and walked off.

Once back at the bungalow, Rishi headed straight to the kitchen.

'Hey, Sunny boy, prepare some basil chicken today. Make it spicy, okay?'

Sunny didn't look pleased with such orders thrust upon

him. The Major never interfered with his selection of menu, why should this upstart boy from the city? Before his frowns translated into words, Saundarya entered the kitchen and, for once, targeted someone other than Sunny. 'Hey! What are you doing in the kitchen? Step out.'

'Just helping our Sunny Leone here, Aunty.'

'The kitchen is not for boys from good families. Only men from lowly backgrounds help in the kitchen. Be a man and step out,' she advised.

Rishi spoke before Sunny could throw his kitchen knife at her. 'True, Aunty. Sunny still needs a lot of training.' He looked at the cook's dagger eyes, now pointed at him. Rishi turned towards the suddenly pleased Saundarya. 'But me? I can slice potatoes while they are up in the air like Rajnikanth.' He tossed a potato upwards to catch it between his palms.

Sunny's anger gave way to laughter. Saundarya frowned, trying to figure out whether the two men were making fun of the great star from her hometown. She decided to change the topic. 'Where had you been? I was looking for you for the evening tea,' she said, as she made to prepare an uttapam for herself.

In one quick stride, Rishi was beside Saundarya, demanding that she share the uttapam with him. She obliged, looking at him strangely. 'I got bored after lunch, Aunty. So I went out for a stroll.'

'At least inform someone,' she ordered, and went her way, after giving Rishi half the uttapam.

'Turncoat!' Sunny abused under his breath, as Rishi finished the uttapam in one mouthful, picked up a piece of fried chicken from a bowl kept on the table, winked at him and disappeared.

✳

Rishi stood in the portico and stared out at the garden for some time. Then, suddenly, he rushed upstairs, picked up his camera and ran down again towards the rear end of the house. Two large rooms stood there in isolation, their doors shut. One had a big lock on it. Here the Major housed his most prized possessions—his collection of cameras. Rishi touched the lock to see if it could be opened. No way! The bulky-looking steel lock was almost as intimidating as its owner. Rishi walked to the other room; this one was just bolted from outside. The room was full of photographs—of landscapes and people, of animals, insects and birds. Every photograph was framed and captioned for display. Every caption was written out in the Major's own handwriting, outlining the details and significance of the shot.

Rishi entered the room. The typical smell of phenyl hit his nose. He walked straight to one of the windows and opened it. Mild rays of the late afternoon sun trickled in. He studied the frames one by one. Almost on an impulse, he picked up three random photographs and placed them on the window sill. One was that of a young Sherpa girl laughing, one captured the face of a middle-aged woman in a desert carrying a huge pot of water on her head, and the last was of a fragile old woman begging outside a temple. He arranged the frames, and looked at their positions through his camera's viewfinder. He inched backwards, focused on the arrangement, found the spot he was looking for and pressed the shutter.

Even before he could inspect the shot, the Major's loud voice echoed in the background.

'What the hell do you think you are doing here?' he roared.

He walked towards Rishi angrily, picked up the photographs and kept them back in their place.

'Do you have any idea how precious these are to me? These are the collections of my entire life. Don't you dare touch these!'

Rishi listened in silence, eyes fixed on his uncle. The raised voice made Saundarya come running; she stood shocked at the door. Rishi did not look at her. His eyes were full of unabashed indifference, unaffected by the man's displeasure. His uncle snatched the DSLR from his hand. The boy did not stop him. He looked at the screen.

For a brief moment, time stopped.

The camera had captured the three photographs in such a way that the women in each were lined up one behind the other. The innocent laughter of the Sherpa girl contrasted with the restless determination of the lady carrying the pot of water, which, in turn, contrasted with the stooped plight of the helpless beggar. The irony of life. Three women in the same frame depicted hope, struggle and despair. The sun's rays filtered in through the gaps between the frames, blurring their edges and glinting off the dark metallic frames.

Stunned, the Major looked up at the boy. The look in Rishi's eyes hadn't changed. He was enjoying his uncle's reaction. Slowly he walked towards him and held out his hand for the camera.

'Anyone can click a photograph, Chacha, but it takes an artist to create a story,' he said softly and walked out of the room.

Late that night, Major General Dhillon sat alone in his room, sipping whisky and looking outside at the dark sal forest.

All these years his duty had taken him across the length and breadth of India. He had travelled while immortalizing many beautiful moments of life in photographs. His peers said he should throw an exhibition. He never took the praises seriously, but somewhere the idea had found a place in his heart. He did think of doing something with the photographs after he retired. This boy, who felt like an imposed addition to his house, had made that secret wish feel meaningless after that one click. His words refused to leave him. *'Anyone can click a photograph, but it takes an artist to create a story.'* The truth hurt. The smooth texture of the whisky seemed to burn his throat as he took another sip.

A gentle tap on the door broke his chain of thought. Irritated, he called out, 'Come in!'

Sunny, the cook, entered nervously. The Major frowned.

'What is it, Sunny?'

'Major Sahab, I have come to tell you a secret,' the cook said, his eyes big.

'What?'

'This Rahul boy...no...er...first promise you will not hurl shoes at me if I tell you everything.'

'Speak up, Sunny. It's too late in the day for drama. You are just messing up my whisky time,' the Major said impatiently.

'Major Sahab, don't tell anyone, but I think this Rahul is Mira Didi's boyfriend.'

He instinctively took two steps backward, in case a shoe actually came flying at the mention of this.

'What!' His employer almost choked on his drink. 'What did you say?'

'Softly, Major Sahab,' he gestured with a finger to his lips.

In the dim light of the room, Sunny's bulging eyes shone with anxious excitement.

'Remember Mira Didi had asked for special food to be prepared when she left for Mumbai? Has Mira Didi ever named any food as her special choice before? No! I have noticed this boy gorges on all the food that Mira Didi got packed while leaving for Mumbai. And then one day, suddenly Mira Didi tells you that a boy is coming to stay here for a few days. Haven't you ever noted how this boy roams around as if this is his ancestral property? He comes into the kitchen, slaps my back and orders me to cook him stuff as if he's known me since birth. He takes the liberty of cracking uncultured jokes at me,' he lowered his voice further, 'He calls me Sunny Leone in front of everyone!' His tone came back to normal. 'I am telling you, Major Sahab, I can smell something fishy. Don't tell me later that I didn't warn you. As your trusted servant, it was my duty to tell you.'

Sunny had said all of this in one breath. The cook's confidence, coupled with the effect of whisky, swirled inside the Major's head. As he sat speechless with deep trenches on his forehead, Sunny took the opportunity to quickly get up, make another drink for his master and flee the room.

Could it be true that Mira was playing games with him? What about Akshat? Was he part of the game as well? It wasn't impossible. He and his daughter only had each other in their life, but they were not really close. Both had kept their distance, burying their thoughts and feelings in their own hearts. If today Mira was not comfortable talking to her father about a boy she liked, he wouldn't blame her.

But Rahul? This boy who called him chacha? This boy who

didn't know anything about formal clothes? Who jumped on to the sofa instead of sitting on it? Who roamed around like a vagabond and smiled like an idiot?

He gulped down the leftover liquid and kept the glass away. Occupied with this new angle to the voluntary exchange programme, the lack of confidence that had gripped him after the camera episode disappeared.

22.

The morning passed in faking apparent calm. A conversation with Rishi the evening before hadn't helped much. The only information he could give her was that Viyaan started work at 2 p.m. and didn't stop till the wee hours of the morning. She convinced Sharat Uncle and Deepti Bua that she was off to visit a school friend. Around 3 p.m. she was standing in front of the under-construction café in Koramangala. She nervously adjusted her shirt, scarf and hair. A man stopped her at the entrance. She found a familiar face behind him from the other day and told him she had probably left her watch inside. She wiped the sweat off her forehead and walked into the chamber where Viyaan was busy crafting the doodles.

Viyaan looked down at her and went back to the wall. Upset with this nonchalance, Mira stood there without a word. Eventually, his voice came from above. 'This is someone's private den. Work is in progress. Would request you not to feel that you can come here any time, just because they let you in once. Nor am I at your disposal just because we have a passing acquaintance.'

People usually didn't talk to Mira like that. She had come there all the way from Cooke's Town, just because she felt she had a responsibility towards clearing up the misunderstanding. Not that she was answerable. But Viyaan's rudeness hurt, a little too much.

Rishi had warned her about this. 'I will tell him when we talk, Browny. He might not even entertain you now. He is a man with a big ego. You don't have to go to him to tender any apology,' he had said. But still she had come. Maybe she shouldn't have. Silently, she adjusted the bag on her shoulder, looked down and walked away. Viyaan frowned as he watched her go. He waited for a moment, climbed down quickly, wiped the colours off his hands with a dirty piece of cloth and jogged to catch up with her.

'Hey!' He caught her in the dark passageway, touching her on the shoulder. She didn't look at him. 'So you came all the ways only to leave?'

No answer.

'I said you can't be entering the place at your whim, but since you had entered anyway, I wasn't deaf.'

Mira's silence was too puzzling. A soft sniff from her nose startled him. Slowly he walked in front to look at her face. She looked away, but could no longer hide the face that had gone dark, and eyes that were now red. Viyaan looked at her, speechless. She tried to walk past him; he blocked the way. She tried to push him away. He took her gently by the elbow and made her stand against the wall. Before she could move, he placed his hands on either side of her, blocking any movement, their bodies close.

Just a day before, she had called this passage terrible. The wall, stained with spit-out betel juice and bird shit, had almost made her puke. Now, with her back resting against the same wall, her mind went blank. The fragrance of his perfume was overpowering, the hair on her forehead quivered as he exhaled. It felt like she was in a trance, with no control over her physical body; his presence so close to hers was like the pull of the infinite, which she could neither react to, nor retract from.

'Are you aware of the damages of using tears as a weapon on a man?' Viyaan whispered.

Both embarrassed and angry, Mira made a brave effort to push him away; she couldn't move him even an inch. She glanced at him and embarrassed herself further as she saw his eyes boring into her.

After a few long seconds, when she didn't know what to do with herself, she looked up again. This time Viyaan lifted his hands off the wall. He fished out a handkerchief from his pocket and offered it to her. She shook her head. All she wanted was to get away from this man. Viyaan put the handkerchief back into his pocket.

'Fine, then, as you wish!'

Before Mira could comprehend what those words meant, his fingers reached for her cheeks and eyes, softly wiping away the tears. She didn't even realize what was happening before it was done. Both his hands inside his pockets now, he stood there enjoying the bemused look on her face.

'Please let me go.' She finally said, almost inaudibly.

This time he stepped back, making way for her. She ran as fast as she could. Viyaan stared after her as she fled in haste, reminiscing how easily she could be picked up like a fallen feather and placed against the wall. In moments of such sudden intimacy, Viyaan would have kissed the woman. For a fleeting second, he did think about pulling her in. But refrained. He somehow couldn't bring himself to do that with Mira. She seemed too conservative, too innocent, too vulnerable.

Her sudden refusal to acknowledge their acquaintance the

day before had felt weird. But her non-response to his caustic words was even more confusing. He had expected her to pick a fight, or at least return the offence. She did reach out to him and apologize last evening; he had ignored it. Whatever may have been her reason for treating him like a stranger before the men the other day, she wasn't the shrewd type. Viyaan did expect her to come back today, but never in his wildest dreams had he thought that she would leave like this. Those large eyes brimming with tears had sent his brain into a frenzy. The feel of her soft, tear-washed skin still lingered on the tips of his rough fingers. He waited in the passageway alone for a few seconds, the last few minutes playing in his mind on loop. Then, in slow steps, he went back to his work.

At the Bahls' flat, the mood couldn't have been more different. The door was open when Mira reached, with shoes strewn across the doorway. She peeped in.

'Sita, come in, quick,' Sharat Uncle called. A few women were seated on the living room sofa; the rest, mostly men, were relaxing on the floor with their kids. Sharat Uncle introduced them as his colleagues and their spouses. 'See how we have trapped the Physics professor today. She is sulking behind the kitchen door.' Sharat Uncle laughed out loud. Mira looked at the other end of the hall. Deepti Bua looked back at her and smiled. She said something inaudible in response to her husband's booming laughter. Sharat Uncle asked her to sit beside him. Deepti Bua soon joined them.

'Don't forget that the girl on your left is an engineering

student,' she warned. 'She will be batting for my camp.'

'Oh!' Sharat Uncle dismissed her hopes. 'She has her heart in literature. Only her feet are in engineering.'

They discussed, analysed and recited Shakespeare, Tennyson, Rossetti and Wordsworth. Some of them read out poems by contemporary poets. And some of them even read out poems they had written themselves. By the time the guests had left, it was quite late. Mira helped Deepti Bua clean up. While arranging the cushions back on the sofa, she smiled at Sharat Uncle in gratitude. Having returned in a foul mood, the evening hadn't let her mull over the insult. 'Thank you for such a beautiful evening, Sir,' she told the elderly man.

He smiled back. 'It was beautiful, wasn't it? Had it been a get-together with Deepti's colleagues, we would have been sitting here discussing the temperature at which water boils while preparing tea.' He laughed aloud but a sharp comment from Deepti Bua startled them both.

'Had my son not inherited this bohemian fondness for useless things from you, he would have been here with us today.' She pointed a finger at her husband. 'You. You are responsible for this.' Before either of them could say a word, she sat down on the sofa and broke down. Mira rushed to her and hugged her.

'You know what your colleague's wife told me in the kitchen? Rishi has uploaded photographs of him painting roadside walls on Facebook. Road. Side. Walls. Can you believe it? And she showed me photographs of him lying down on the footpath, taking a nap. Thank God I have suspended my Facebook account—I don't have to see what my son is putting himself through.' Her voice was wet with tears. Sharat Uncle stood there beside her miserably. The cheerful evening was suddenly lost.

'What happened to him, Ma'am?' Mira asked softly.

Deepti Bua sobbed. 'He doesn't understand. He just doesn't. His pursuits will take him nowhere. He is just out there, spoiling his life. We, the parents, are cast aside to lead a lonely life. Everyone has their children standing by them. They talk proudly about them building their lives intelligently. But the only thing we have to talk about at any gathering are term papers and schedules. What have we done to deserve this?'

This went on for a few minutes. Mira got her a glass of water while Sharat Uncle sat down, resigned. Mira spoke, very softly, to both of them, when Deepti Bua seemed calmer. 'Did you ever tell him this, Ma'am?'

Deepti Bua shook her head. 'No. Why should we? Why should we let him know our weakness if he doesn't care? At the end of leading a life of repute, we don't deserve to beg. Not even to our own son.'

Choosing her next words cautiously, Mira said, 'Don't beg, Ma'am. But just let him know…in your own way. Maybe he suffers the same loneliness as you do? Who knows if he, too, has something to tell you when you open your hearts to him? Just try it, Ma'am. You have nothing to lose. He is your son.' She stopped. Both Deepti Bua and Sharat Uncle were now looking at her. She shrugged.

Deepti Bua got up and walked slowly past them into her room. The bad taste in her mouth from earlier in the evening was coming back. She shouldn't have gone to Koramangala. She hated her foolishness. Miserably, she walked inside and sat on her bed. She didn't realize when the lights went out in the living room.

Late in the night, by the light of a table lamp, Mira sat on a chair, hugging her knees. She hid her face in them. She wanted to go back to Mumbai, where the brother guarded her like a wall. In his absence, she felt exposed.

A few days back, Rishi had called her, sounding terribly upset. 'Why didn't you tell me about Shiraz, Browny?' he had charged.

'I didn't feel like.'

'How could you not?'

'Till you knew, Shiraz was alive in your heart, Rishi. I didn't want to change that. He was your hero.'

The brother had gone silent. She knew how his heart must have bled with that information. She wanted to sit beside him and share the pain. Deepti Bua's outburst that evening was equally disturbing. She felt sad, and prayed that things would settle down between mother and son.

A soft touch on her head made her look up. Sharat Uncle smiled at her affectionately. She straightened up. 'I think you were our daughter in some other life.'

Mira smiled back. 'Why another life? I am your daughter in this life too.' She felt tired and somewhat drained while saying it. It was unfair that they didn't know who she was.

Sharat Uncle kissed her head. 'God bless you,' he muttered.

'Is Ma'am fine?' she asked.

'Yes. She just slept.' Sharat Uncle paused. 'Sorry about that. Deepti has this habit of throwing up hyper reactions all too suddenly. Don't remember this evening.'

'I won't,' she assured him. He left.

Fatigued, she hit the bed. Late at night her phone beeped. She opened her sleepy eyes to pull the mobile phone towards her. A WhatsApp message said, 'Curzon Court. Loudin Café. Noon. Come. Else I know where Murthy lives.'

Disgusted and intrigued at the same time, she threw the phone under a heap of pillows. He had no right to force her. And what a tone to invite someone out! Was she his vain sketch, that he felt free to draw a line wherever he wanted? She wouldn't go. She tried to go back to sleep. Her mobile beeped again from under the pillows. Another WhatsApp message gave her the directions.

'Why can't he sleep when the rest of the world does?' she fumed.

Problem No. 3,319: I'm not going!

23.

A sixteen-minute walk from the house got him to Mall Road. He stood there in the early-morning light with his camera. The sun had lit up the snow-clad mountains in the distance. He took in the serene beauty of the place and started walking again, clicking anything that caught his fancy on the way, anything that had a latent story to tell, a beauty that could only be visually acknowledged, never verbally expressed. One of his random clicks caught a figure in the background, seated not too far away. He zoomed in. A woman on the staircase of the Shimla Public Library, with something in her lap. He squinted in the direction. She was reading a book. Two more voluminous books lay beside her; a thick plait ran down her back and brushed the step on which she sat. He pressed the shutter of his camera. Her lean figure, with the picturesque backdrop, made for a splendid shot. He walked towards her and cleared his throat. The girl turned and smiled. Quickly she pulled her dupatta up to cover her head.

'Shabnam!' Rishi asked surprised. 'What are you doing here?'

She frowned. 'You are standing on my land, Mr Rahul Pandey. That question is for me to ask.'

He handed her the camera. She scrolled through the images. Rishi turned to inspect one of the books on the staircase. The cover read IAS in big, bold fonts.

'Are you preparing for the IAS?' Rishi didn't know whether he was happy or shocked, or both.

'Yes, I am.'

'I actually never asked what you were doing. Please tell me,' he urged.

'I am a student of Lady Shri Ram College in Delhi. Botany Honours. And secretly studying for this.' She smiled.

'Why secretly?'

'What if I can't make it?' The question seemed to be humouring him. Her voice had the confidence, her face shone with conviction.

'You will make it. Photographers can foresee things.' Rishi raised his hand like a saint. Shabnam laughed.

'You are here for the holidays?' he asked.

'Yes.'

He sat down two steps below her. 'Why were you walking with that pile of clothes the other day? I thought they were meant to be washed. You guys offer laundry services?'

'Not laundry, but Ammi picks up clothes to be pressed. I help her when I am here.'

'That's all you do for a living?' Rishi could not help probing. A girl from this family was ambitious enough to prepare for one of the toughest examinations in India! Admiration and curiosity swept through him.

'Shabbir Chachu drives tourists to different destinations. When I am here, I help too. I take them around for local sightseeing. Ammi cooks at a hotel. I do a part-time job in college. Chachi stitches clothes. All included, we manage to pull it off.'

Rishi's eyes had grown big. 'You can drive? You have a driving licence?'

'What's so strange about it?' Her expression told him this was not the first time she had surprised someone with that information.

Rishi grew serious. 'Shiraz must be very proud of you, wherever he is.' He looked at the sky. Memories like tattered clouds were being teased by the passing breeze. They pushed back but emerged again, from the same epicenter of tender rumination. Shiraz used to compose folk songs. Even the most mundane things from everyday life were transformed into magical elements in his songs—sunshine, snow-clad hills, the shiver of winter mornings, waterfalls, the star-studded sky. And the marigolds. No one knew why Shiraz was so fond of marigolds. But he had told Rishi once.

'Shabnam, my little fairy, loves marigolds. When she was a few months old, I had exhausted all my money and didn't have anything to give her for Eid. I took home some marigolds. I swayed them in front of her and she chuckled. She was so happy. Since then, I have been growing these flowers. As long as my marigolds are safe and blooming bright, my daughter is happy.'

Shiraz protected the marigolds as if he were securing smiles for his daughter. Where was Shiraz now? Rishi didn't realize that his eyes had brimmed over. Shabnam brought him back from his trance. Her soft reassurance of 'Abbu loved you' let free a drop that he had so obstinately been holding on to. Rishi quickly wiped his eyes.

A few moments passed in pensive silence. Shabnam quietly turned the pages of her book. Rishi eventually got up. 'I have to leave. You want to sit here?' Shabnam looked at him. 'If you come with me, I will get to ride your cycle.'

'Only for a short distance,' Shabnam warned, as they walked to where the cycle was parked behind the church. He sat on the cycle waiting for her. She arranged the books on her lap and adjusted herself on the rear seat.

'Do you cover your head even when you are in college?' Rishi asked as they rode.

'No. Here Ammi gets offended if I walk around without a veil.'

They laughed about things, discussed a few others, and after a while, Rishi got off, leaving Shabnam to ride the cycle alone the rest of the way. He walked on, turning around again and again to look at Shabnam pedalling away. What a fantastic woman! She deserved to be the daughter of Shiraz.

Unmindfully, he opened the gate to the bungalow. Immediately he sensed something was brewing.

Since he had woken up, Major General Dhillon had been looking for the 'boy'. He had found that he had disappeared, as always, without telling anyone. Angry with this kind of irresponsible behaviour, he had walked into Rishi's room. The sight of the ill-kept room only irked him further. The guy had even kept his laptop open on the desk. He went to flip it closed. At the touch of his finger, the screen saver danced to life. It was a photograph of Mira. Shocked, and Sunny's suspicions vehemently confirmed, he slapped the screen shut.

'This boy, of all people?' he thought miserably. 'Weird, and with no sense of decorum? Unkempt, roaming around in slippers, how will this boy ever match up to Mira? He is a walking, living embarrassment. How will I introduce this boy as my future son-in-law? And that Akshat! Scoundrel! He is supporting them, instead of discouraging them?'

The man wanted to bang his head on the wall. But then he remembered the photograph the boy had clicked a day before. He had to admit the boy had fine creative wisdom. Maybe he wasn't that bad, after all. With a little help from him, things could just turn around. He cleared his throat heavily and decided he would tailor this boy to suit Mira.

'Is that why Mira sent him here? So I can take him to task and change some of the habits she can't? Not impossible.' Finally, the Major was smiling. His daughter was more intelligent than he had thought. 'She wants us to understand each other. Akshat confirmed that the boy has a great future. Now the only thing to do is develop his personality. He needs to grow out of his childish actions and get serious. I will take this up strictly from now on. Enough fun this boy has had,' he told himself.

And no. No one must know about this. Not yet. He'd have to tell Sunny that he was an idiot and that his assumptions were bogus.

As Rishi walked past the garden, he found the Major standing stiffly on the patio, watching him. He sat on the stairs to take his shoes off and looked up, confused. 'What, Chacha?' he asked, trying to put his finger on the burning issue this morning.

Chacha! The older man fumed. 'Call me Major.' He reminded him curtly. 'Where had you been?'

'Just walking around to see the place. What's the point of being somewhere if you have to go back before you have got to know everything about it?' He tried to smile, but the moustache still looked grim.

'Didn't anyone ever tell you that you must inform people before you leave? You are new here. We have a responsibility. We are answerable if you are in trouble. What's your problem?'

'Fine, then. Usually when I leave, people are still sleeping in this house. I will wake up everyone up from now on,' he pronounced.

The Major opened his mouth to say something, but Rishi didn't allow him to speak. 'Now don't say that I must go out at a time when it is convenient for everyone. You don't choose the time you have to go for duty. Don't ask me to choose either. It is the same for everyone. We are off when work calls.' He sounded serious, showing him his camera.

The Major fell silent. This boy had just reminded him of his sister, Deepti. She was the only person on earth who would argue with him like that, with unexpected but impeccable logic. He forced himself to concentrate on this pain in front. He was still sitting there, humming now.

'What have you thought of doing with your life? What are your plans? What bread would a degree in Arts fetch you?' He hurled the questions all at the same time.

Rishi stopped humming. His mother's voice. His mother's questions. The same intellectual arrogance. Irritation surged inside him. He tried his best to suppress it.

'I want to enjoy life. I want to ensure that whatever I am doing with each passing moment documents a beautiful journey and creates memories. So, basically, I want the life of Virat Kohli. I want to live it in style.' He waited for a ruthless, judgemental reaction. He closed his eyes. Perhaps this was the smog Shiraz had once referred to.

His uncle's voice boomed, heavy with displeasure. 'Are you

serious? Virat Kohli? Try being Sachin Tendulkar instead. Put in some hard work and honesty. You want to enjoy life—and that's all you have to tell me when I ask you about your career plans? Do you remotely realize how impractical this is?'

Rishi looked up again, his eyes intense. 'Just because you couldn't enjoy your life doing what you wanted, you think no one else should? You chose your life, I chose mine.' He shrugged.

'You chose your life? What life? To roam around like a vagabond, clicking photographs?' his uncle asked angrily.

The nephew smiled in sarcasm. 'Given a choice, you would have loved to do that too. Just that you didn't know how to do it.' Before his uncle could offend him any more, he invited him to follow. Reluctantly, the Major went with him.

Once in his room, Rishi opened his laptop. He punched in his password, selected a folder and clicked on an ad layout he had been working on lately for Viyaan's team. He turned the screen towards the Major. 'You know what the market value of this photograph will be, once it has been processed?' The Major looked at the photograph and then flatly back at him. His eyes popped when Rishi told him. 'It will fetch more than ₹3 lakh.'

The Major looked at the boy in disbelief. 'You mean each photograph you click fetches you more than ₹3 lakh?'

'No, that's not correct.' Rishi laughed. 'Everything that nature gives you is raw. You have to process it, cook it, enrich it with flavours and spices, and yet make it digestible. Just clicking with a camera might be as useless as uncooked rice. I have to explain it to the audience so it can be of some use. That's my work. Call me a chef or an artist.' He grinned. 'Or just call me Kohli. Work like you are having a blast with the bat, rather than worshipping the bat like Tendulkar.'

Silently, the Major got up to leave. The boy here wasn't as idiot, as he had first thought. He had mettle. Akshat was right. Maybe his daughter had not made the wrong choice, after all. He was inwardly debating the pros and cons of this strange boy's personality when a hand from behind brought him back to reality. Shocking his uncle once again, Rishi put his arm around the Major's shoulder. The Major jerked it off.

'You know what? You are nagging, but not a bully.' The boy smiled again like a fool. His reserve, which had seemed impressive till a second ago, was lost again. The Major clenched his teeth as his system processed the words 'bully' and 'nagging'. He kept walking. The boy walked with him, unwilling to leave. 'Stop, Chacha. I have a request,' he said earnestly.

'It is Major.' The uncle corrected him again. 'What is it now?'

'I want to see your collection of cameras.' The smile had disappeared and his eyes were twinkling with excitement. 'Please.'

The Major surveyed him from top to bottom. It felt weird how this boy switched between his fiery and laid-back personalities with such ease. One moment he was a ball of passion, dismissing every logic and putting his point across with an urgency like his life rested on its pointed edge. He then spoke as if no one was even qualified to understand what he was talking about. But with the very next utterance, he transformed into this strange, comical character who laughed loudly and dressed clumsily, irritating the hell out of everyone around. His interest in the Major's camera collection somewhat softened him.

'I'll show you sometime,' he said.

'Major Sahab,' Rishi called out from behind. The uncle turned. 'Thanks.' The boy smiled.

'For what?' He frowned.

'At least you asked about my career,' the boy smiled. 'Usually people don't. They just form opinions. Are you really so fair with everyone in your life, or I am a special beneficiary?'

Not sure what exactly the boy had asked, which unsettled the Major, he turned and walked off without a response.

No, he hadn't been a fair person, he thought. He had been unfair to everyone close to him. He hadn't been a good father or a good brother. He had served his country with great honesty— the national flag was his biggest identity. It gave him a decent living, a life of reputation. He never questioned the obvious. He felt he had led the life of a real man. But some corner of his heart today said that this boy was braver than he had ever been. He had courage, he didn't care what others had to say about him. Perhaps he enjoyed more freedom than this country did even after 72 years of independence!

24.

Mira unmindfully took the cup of tea Sharat Uncle handed to her that morning. It had almost become a ritual for him to bring her a cup on the balcony after he had bantered with his wife enough. Over tea, Sharat Uncle discussed philosophy, psychology, poetry and literature. At times Mira felt that he used his knowledge of difficult subjects to hide from simple things he was uncomfortable with.

His wife teased, 'He is so obsessed with teaching that he won't even spare the poor engineering student. Too insecure having to share the apartment with two women of science.' Sharat Uncle would retort that Deepti Bua could speak so much because she was empowered by language, which was literature. He warned that she must treat literature with more respect.

'Just check whether there are chilli flakes in the tea,' Sharat Uncle said as he handed her the cup. 'Deepti has been especially sharp with her tongue today.' Deepti Bua overheard this from the kitchen and said something inaudible in protest. Sharat Uncle winked at Mira.

'Is it fine?' he asked again.

Mira took a sip. 'No, Sir, I am not going.'

'Where?'

Startled out of her thoughts, Mira fumbled, 'No, sorry. I had been thinking of something else.'

'And what is that?'

'A friend...no...no...not really a friend...just like that... nothing...asked me out. I don't feel like,' she said nervously.

'Why wouldn't you like to meet a friend?' Sharat Uncle looked surprised. 'This is the time, girl. Go and meet people, have fun.' He studied her for a while, then looked at the kitchen and leant in closer. 'Is it a boyfriend?'

'No, no, not at all. Impossible. This is a madman...I mean, not mad, but weird. No boyfriend.' She tried to brush off the thought, but her face had already gone red.

'Then this madman is interested in you. Who is he?' he whispered.

Reluctantly, Mira confided in him. 'Yesterday when I went out, I met that artist at Murthy Uncle's café... I didn't mean to...'

'Viyaan Iyer?' Sharat Uncle almost shouted and then lowered his voice. 'He asked you out, and you are thinking whether you want to go? He is a steal, lady. Handsome and successful. Go for it. I remember what a cut-throat deal Murthy had to strike to get him on this project. He had promised himself that if he ever opened a café, the interiors would be done only by this Iyer guy. He waited endlessly till he got a yes from him.' He chuckled.

'Really?' Mira looked at her uncle. 'Isn't he in the kind of profession that you don't approve of?' She paused to gauge the uncle's reaction to her words. 'My family is very conservative. If they know I am going out with a man, that, too, someone who writes on walls...' she stopped abruptly, looking at Sharat Uncle from the corner of her eyes. His natural mirth had gone.

'They won't. Nothing is more important than success, girl. Just go and spend time with someone different. Come back with an experience. Learn something new. And tell me about it.' He tried to smile.

'How far is Curzon Court from here?'

'Don't worry. I will take Deepti for some shopping today. We will drop you on the way.' He smiled again. 'Tell me everything about the meeting when we are back.'

Mira smiled too. 'Should I talk to him about your son? Maybe, if Viyaan Iyer wants, he can help with his career. Ma'am will get some peace of mind.' She tried to take a chance.

'No.' Sharat Uncle's voice had suddenly grown serious. 'Never. He took a plunge. Either he carves his own way or he rots. No one will make his path for him through references.'

Mira smiled. These people didn't know that their son was already working with Viyaan Iyer and that it was Viyaan who had approached him with an offer. She felt proud of her brother again.

Seated by the window of Loudin Café, Mira fiddled with the end of her dupatta, hoping Viyaan wouldn't come. Maybe he would get stuck with something at work. Maybe his car would have a breakdown. Maybe he would suddenly remember some other obligation. She kept an eye on her mobile, almost praying that this meeting would get called off. But no such text came. Viyaan Iyer, however, did.

He casually tossed his glares inside the car and walked towards the café entrance. Any guy would think a hundred times before selecting that parrot-green T-shirt, Mira thought. His tattoos were visible through the short sleeves and open buttons at the neck. He spotted Mira, smiled and walked towards her. She crossed her hands across her chest, her nails digging into her skin. It hurt, but that was nothing compared to her dramatic tears yesterday.

Why, God, why the hell did she have to cry? Why did this man have to see her like that? What must he be thinking? The brother hugs and the sister cries? What a nonsensical farce! She wanted to disappear and not face him again. But it was too late.

Viyaan came towards her in long strides. He threw his bag on the seat in front and sat down beside her. By reflex, Mira slid into the corner, so their bodies didn't touch. He ignored her reaction. Before she could open her mouth, Viyaan spoke, looking her in the eye.

'Listen. I don't carry anything personal when I am working. That includes my mobile, and also the friends I may have. You know why? Because it distracts me. Just like I haven't been able to crack a single design since you left yesterday. Distractions are a curse in my profession. So, sometimes, when I am rude, please understand that I am addressing a curse, not necessarily the person standing in front.'

He paused as she blushed.

'Since I am starving, let's order something.'

Mira wasn't hungry, but she ordered anyway to avoid any more conversation than was necessary. She tried to explain her behaviour from the evening before. 'See...yesterday...I wasn't...I mean, of course I was...but...well, I'm sorry. I didn't mean to appear so touchy.' She almost gasped, having completed the sentence with abnormal awkwardness.

'I could see that,' Viyaan said with a mischievous smile. 'The moment I touched you, you fled.'

Thoroughly embarrassed, Mira looked away. She tried to say something. It wasn't audible.

'So, Sita Sharma. What is this story? How come Rishi's father does not know you?' Viyaan asked.

Mira turned to look at him. 'How do you know he is Rishi's father?'

'Rishi's CV said he was the son of Sharat Bahl. Murthy said that the name of his friend, who was accompanied by Sita Sharma, was Sharat Bahl. You having two Sharat Bahls in your life, that, too, in Bengaluru, would be too much of a coincidence.' He shrugged.

'It's a long story. We'll talk about it some other time.' Mira dismissed his curiosity, unwilling to discuss her family issues with Viyaan. 'But please don't tell them that you know Rishi. That day I was scared that you would suddenly call me Mira and name Rishi...so...' Her voice faded away.

'Where is Rishi?' He asked after taking a sip of his coffee.

'Shimla.'

'...Which is your place. People at your house don't recognize him either. This is a thriller. You guys must be criminals.' He laughed.

A few people at the café glanced at them. Mira felt everyone there knew she had cried the evening before and that Viyaan was laughing remembering it. She shrank. 'I am sorry,' she whispered.

'For what?' Viyaan was sitting relaxed on the sofa. She didn't know what to say. He turned to take a closer look at her. She was still fiddling with her dupatta, pressing tightly into the corner of the sofa so the distance between them was as much as possible.

Not that he wasn't nervous, but he knew better than to show it. Her face disclosed everything.

It was the first time that Viyaan had been rude to someone and felt bad about it. He was known to be impulsive and temperamental. His portfolio had as many records of tears as reports of his genius. He had never cared. But he couldn't be as indifferent with this girl. And that felt uncomfortable. Something wasn't very clear. Something wasn't usual. The more he got nervous, the more he tried to take control of the situation. And the more it went out of his hands. Her distance made him uncomfortable. He wanted to reach out and comfort her; he wanted to touch her restless fingers; he wanted to pull her closer; he wanted to bring his face right next to hers, lock their eyes and assure her that everything was fine. But any attempt to do so would be disastrous. He got up instead and sat on the sofa on the other side of the table to face her. Surprised with his sudden change of position, Mira tried to shift. Viyaan quickly put his hands on hers, resting on the table, and rendered her motionless.

'You think I am the devil, don't you? Have you complained to your darling brother already?'

Confused, she shook her head, conscious of the warmth of his hands on hers. She wanted them free. The strength imposed on her, though, seemed to be in no hurry, neither did it acknowledge her discomfort. The voice hypnotized her. She looked up at the eyes in front.

'Then why don't you talk to me?' Viyaan's impatience showed blatantly, shocking the man himself. He tried to remember some frail, half-forgotten voices that had called him 'ruthless', 'mean' and 'cold-blooded' in the past. This afternoon he was behaving more like them and less like himself. That freaked him out. 'If you were unhappy with what I said, why didn't you say anything? How could you just accept it and move on? Am I a stone that bruises your feet and you still don't bother to stop?'

Viyaan knew that people protested against his nonchalance. They complained, got angry, abused prophesied that his arrogance would one day result in his fall. But he ignored them all and walked away only with whatever mattered most. People never mattered to him. The more you got affected by them, the deeper you dug your own grave. People could never belong to anyone. They were like tides that swelled when the moon shone bright. Work was his parent, friend, sibling and his only lover.

More than anything else last evening, Mira's silence had felt unsettling. She had discarded him like rotten fruit and walked out on him. He had run behind her to find out why. What had happened thereafter, he couldn't comprehend. Since then, those large, teary eyes just wouldn't leave him alone. He tried to shoo them away all night, waiting to meet her in the morning and clarify this. But clarification was the last thing happening across the table. This was even more confusing. She tried to pull her hands away once again. This time he laced his fingers through hers and held them even tighter. Red in the face, she looked around to see if anyone was watching them. With a vengeance Viyaan lifted his other hand, turning her face towards him. She blushed at the sudden touch, and her eyes widened, both concerned and cornered.

'Look at me,' Viyaan hissed. 'And concentrate. This is between us. Others don't matter.'

Mira wasn't sure what that meant. His eyes wanted something from her. Something very scary. Yet, something very tempting. Viyaan gently pulled her hand towards himself, on which he had full control now. He guided her palm to touch his cheek, nose, mouth and neck. She pulled it back forcefully, almost breathless now. She wanted to run, but her legs wouldn't move. Neither would his gaze from her face.

When she came back home, Sharat Uncle, as usual, sat in his library, reading. Deepti Bua was busy cleaning a shelf. Sharat Uncle peeped out from behind his book and gestured to ask how it went. She smiled and reached out to Deepti Bua to help. Together they cleaned the shelves that were dusty, wiped the racks with a piece of cloth and put the books back again. They discussed funny things that happened in their colleges and classrooms, giggling like kids. Mira told her of a typical day at her engineering college. Deepti Bua had her own stories about students and colleagues.

Sharat Uncle looked at them from his chair, his attention now diverted considerably from the book in hand. He didn't remember when last he had seen his wife so natural. Deepti had always wanted a girl. When Anil, her brother, had had a daughter, she had showered her with everything she could on earth. She had pampered Anil's little daughter more than she had her own son. After Anil and Deepti fought and refused to see each other again, it left a permanent void in her heart, from which she could never recover. Spending time with this girl was perhaps healing her on some level. Without interfering, he went back to his book. But he couldn't continue for too long. His ears caught a few words and he looked up.

A few old albums had been discovered while cleaning the library shelves. Mira was flipping through those. They introduced a very young Deepti and Sharad when they were in college. Some of the photographs showed them holding hands. The aunt blushed and tried to snatch the album away, but Mira wouldn't let go. As they both tried to pull the album away from the other, giggling like children, an envelope fell to the floor. Anticipating more lovey-dovey photographs inside, they both reached for it. Mira swiftly opened the envelope and poured out its contents. What scattered on the floor silenced both of them. The sudden quiet stood in stark contrast to the fun they were having just a few seconds ago.

The photographs, dog-eared with time, showed the hills in black and white, with a well-built man in uniform, holding a girl by her hand and a little boy on his lap.

Mira asked the obvious, as innocently as she could. 'Who are they, Ma'am?' She tried to retain the mirthful look on her face, but Deepti Bua had gone pale. She looked desperately at her husband, begging for him to come to her rescue.

'Family friends,' Sharat Uncle said, hoping that the chapter would be closed there. That didn't happen. Mira looked at both of them, her eyes studying their faces a bit longer than usual. She flipped through some more photographs and picked one up for a closer look.

'I know this person,' she said, startling both the husband and the wife. 'Isn't this Major General Anil Dhillon? His daughter is in our college. In fact, she is my batchmate.'

Sharat Uncle left his book and walked towards them, sitting down on the floor beside the scattered photographs. He looked at his wife. Both of them had gone abnormally quiet, their attention fixed on Mira. 'Mira Dhillon. I think she is doing Computer Science,' the girl said, looking at them.

Deepti Bua seemed to be in a state of shock. Sharat Uncle started asking questions. How did she look? Did she have a photograph of Mira Dhillon? How was Mira in studies? Was she friends with her? How much did she know of Major Dhillon? How did he look now? At some point, Deepti Bua left to serve lunch. She had grown quiet and withdrawn.

The day went by with few words from her and more questions from Sharat Uncle. Every time he asked something, Deepti Bua would listen keenly but never say anything.

Late in the night, when Sharat Uncle had gone to sleep, she heard her aunt crying again in the living room. Mira didn't move an inch from her bed. What she had touched upon that evening wasn't so uncomplicated. The revival of relationships after sixteen years would have its own repercussions and take its own time. She allowed her aunt to let out part of her repressed anguish uninterfered. She deserved the privacy.

In that shared isolation, Mira, too, was finally left to ponder the most bizarre afternoon of her life.

When he had dropped her, Viyaan had opened his arm for a hug. Despite knowing well that this could be dangerous, she hadn't been able to avoid it. As she had moved closer to him, his hands had touched her back softly. His smell, his warmth, had engulfed Mira. She couldn't withdraw as fast as she thought she would. But when she finally did, for a brief second, they had looked at each other, his hands still around her waist. She had pushed herself backwards before they could progress any further. Viyaan had passed her a shy smile, perhaps for the first time in his life, and got back to the steering wheel.

25.

'Your dad has freaked out completely, Browny.'

'What has he done now? The other day he told me over the phone that he wants to cut you to shape, so that you become more responsible.' Mira tried not to laugh.

'You are telling me now? Where were you all this while? Running around trees with my boss?'

Mira looked around to see if someone was prying on their conversation. 'Shut up, moron,' she whispered.

Rishi chuckled. 'What's going on, Browny?'

She sounded dazed. 'I have no idea.'

'Then who has an idea? Saundarya Ma?'

'Every time I decide that I don't want to see him again, I end up going anyway. He takes over after that. I come back feeling like a brainless idiot.'

'You enjoy his company, don't you?' This had no answer from his sister.

Rishi frowned. He came back to the Major. 'You know what your father did yesterday? I found the watchman wearing my orange T-shirt and walking around happily. I went back to my wardrobe and found most of my T-shirts missing. They have been replaced with new sets of formals. I asked the Major what was happening. He said a man looks like a man in his formals. He was just so unapologetic! Now am I supposed to wear those ties he brought for me while shooting? This is ridiculous.'

Mira laughed aloud. 'Handle it yourself, Rishi. I can't do much from here. By the way, Sunny is livid you called him Sunny Leone.'

'Oh, please! That crook has watched all her films. Can you beat that?' Rishi shrugged. 'What's happening with the professors?' he asked finally.

Mira told him about the recent developments.

'Excellent move, Browny,' he exclaimed. 'Maybe I should plan something similar.'

They hung up after they had given each other due updates. He looked around. Some of his favourite T-shirts and three-quarter pants were gone. What he had still left with him felt stupid. He sat resigned, with one leg on the table, opened a bottle of water and took loud, clumsy gulps from it. He choked, as a voice behind him suddenly roared.

'Is this the way to sit? Sit properly, right now.'

Rishi got up, really irritated. 'Is this the way to call someone? From behind? I could have died had the water gone into my lungs!'

His concerns were ignored. 'Come, let's go for a walk.'

'Walk? With you?'

'Is that a problem?' The Major's eyebrows shot up in his forehead.

'Yes. You are the ultimate definition of a bore.'

The Major clenched his teeth to control the bout of anger that swelled inside him. He glared at the boy.

'Come on, don't tell me no one said that to you before.' Rishi had started enjoying himself again.

Had he not been·his daughter's suitor, the Major would have

shot him then and there. But he didn't want to be the typical father who created a ruckus about accepting his daughter's choice. For the first time, his daughter wanted something from him. He wouldn't violate that. There had to be a patient way of dealing with this pain of a boy. Remembering the strange key to this weird lock, he put his hand inside his pocket and took out a metal object. 'You want it or not?' The boy's expression changed.

Rishi stared at the key to the camera room in the Major's raised hand and fumbled. 'This is the worst kind of cheap blackmail I have ever seen in my life.'

The Major smiled sarcastically to celebrate his victory. 'I am waiting downstairs.' He left, happy with his intelligent move. You have to catch the bull by its horns, he thought.

Rishi threw his head back in frustration, picked up his mobile phone and stepped out. This man had even thrown away his slippers. A pair of sports shoes and black formal shoes were placed near the door. He groaned.

They jogged through the road, talking less. The nephew had to admit that his uncle's lungs were in extremely good shape. They didn't stress under the exertion, while he was panting after just a kilometre and a half. They stopped at a roadside tea stall. The aroma of ginger felt comforting after the exertion.

'Pay for your own tea,' the Major snarled.

'You planned this run out of the blue. In fact, you called me for a walk and made me run. You pay the penalty.' Rishi got up and picked up another glass. The uncle scowled at him; the boy didn't care.

On their way back, the uncle asked about his career plans again. This time the boy looked serious.

'Have you heard of Buffers?' Rishi asked.

'Yes,' the uncle said immediately. 'When a video takes time to load, it is called buffering.'

The nephew burst out laughing, as the uncle looked offended, wondering what was incorrect about what he said.

'Buffers Inc. is an ad agency. They are huge, with offices in eighteen countries. I will be interning with them when the summer is over.'

Embarrassed, the Major opened the gate and entered the house. 'Let's go to the camera room,' he said. Rishi followed in silence.

The collection was exotic. Cameras from different countries, different ages, and with different looks and features were laid out in display. They were perfectly maintained, with not a speck of dust anywhere. Rishi picked some out of their cases and inspected them. The Major showed him the operation techniques. For once, Rishi listened without a word. Every history that was discussed, every feature that was demonstrated, he absorbed with full attention. The Major noticed his focus. In all these days, this was the first time that nephew and uncle bonded like disciples pursuing a common discipline.

After dinner that evening, they sat down together on the veranda. The Major narrated stories from his life. The places he had been to, the people he had met, the things he had done, the lengths he had gone to at times to click an object of interest, and the way he had researched and sourced the cameras for his collection, all in the absence of the Internet. Sometime in between, Sunny lit a bonfire in the garden. The Major sipped his whisky as he spoke. He offered a glass to the boy; he refused.

They both stared blankly at the bonfire.

This felt like a recap of the past! Just that all the people who used to share these moments together were scattered. After years, nephew and uncle seemed to have come back to revive something surreal. But one didn't know what was happening and the other wasn't sure where it was all heading. Rishi suppressed an urge to hug the Major. Despite all the nastiness he threw at him, he softened as the evening explored a different side to the uncle. A few pegs down, his uncle spoke unbarred, wanting to say more. God knows since when he had stored these words inside his heart. That evening he bared them to someone he didn't even know enough, and neither appreciated, but a shared interest and undefined deprivation egged him on.

At some point, Rishi took the gamble.

'Why are you so lonely? Where's your family?' he asked in an unusually soft voice.

Intoxicated eyes looked up to verify the innocence behind the question, but couldn't gauge any answer from the boy's demeanour. Complications in relationships set lucid by the effect of liquor, the uncle braved answers he had not even admitted to himself.

'I didn't ever have a family. I had a wife; I had parents; I have a daughter and a sister. But I wasn't close to anyone. They left, eventually...all of them...one by one. When you don't water your plants, they die.'

'You didn't stop them?'

'What right did I have? I couldn't give them any happiness. Because I didn't have it with me. They are better off without me.'

'Why do you say that?' Rishi probed.

'If that weren't true, they would have come back.' Major General Dhillon drained his glass. He picked up the bottle to make himself another drink. Rishi stopped him.

'Don't.'

'I am not drunk yet. In the Army we are trained to be alert, always in our senses. A few pegs can do nothing.' He tried to smile.

'You are stressed. Give yourself the time you deserve. Talk to me. Stop avoiding the conversation,' Rishi insisted.

'Why do you want to know?'

'I can see that you have everything just around the corner; you just aren't taking the turn.'

'How?' The Major leant forward.

Rishi bent forward in his chair too, to make himself distinctly audible. 'Don't you see that you have blocked others from reaching out to you? Maybe those who left you are just a call away. They are scared to come to you. They are scared that you will discard them. Why don't you just take that first step?'

'I can't.' The Major sat back, resigned. His eyes seemed blank.

Rishi got up quietly to leave. That was enough for the day. The uncle called out to him from behind.

'Here, you can keep this. Visit the room when you need to.' He held up the key to the room downstairs.

Rishi smiled. This man had a strange way of expressing affection. No kind words, just rewards! He knew this was something he hadn't ever given anyone, not even his own daughter.

'That's yours,' he asserted. 'You keep it. I will take it from you sometimes and enter the room with your permission.' He left.

*

Early the next morning, Rishi set out to find Shabnam. He found her in front of their house, performing namaz. Rishi stood behind a tree and watched. Years ago he had seen her mother doing this in the same place. He had asked endless questions on why she covered her head and body with the cloth, why she joined her palms, raising them near the face, why she touched the ground with her head. Shiraz had never shut him off, saying it was her ritual for offering prayers.

'She is seeking inner happiness,' he had said.

'Isn't it through the magic entrance?' Rishi had pointed towards his door.

'It's everywhere, spread across the universe. But you have to crave it,' Shiraz had whispered with his characteristic calm. 'She has closed her eyes so that she doesn't see anything that can steer her away from her focus. She has covered herself so that no monster from this part of the world can touch her as she seeks the path of the divine. She has raised her hands with promises to give as much as she takes. The bow is to thank the cosmos for allowing her to be a miniscule part of its enormous whole.'

This morning, as Shabnam repeated the rituals, Rishi heard Shiraz saying the same things again, his voice still distinct in his memory.

When she was done, he raised his hand and waved. She gestured to him to head to a spot a little distance from the house. Rishi walked till there. She followed, wheeling her cycle beside her. Before she could say anything, he pleaded to Shabnam, taking her by surprise, 'Please get me a pair of slippers. He has thrown them away.'

Rishi explained the Major's new form of torture. Shabnam's laughter sent ripples through the air. The veil fell off her head.

Today her hair was not tied into a plait. It fanned out across her shoulders. She looked like a wild forest, unplanned and beautiful. Rishi forgot to press the shutter of his camera. Some pictures leave impressions on the mind. They come back like a gush of water, soaking you from the inside out. You try to touch them and they disappear into thin air.

Rishi tried to shake this impression out of his head. It wouldn't go. Quietly, he looked away.

'What do people do for leisure here? You can't be trekking every day. No malls, no pubs, what are the ways you have fun?' he asked to divert his attention.

'In Shimla only honeymooners are allowed to have fun.' She smiled brightly. 'Otherwise, you have Shimla Times Café near Mall Road. It has live music playing and quite a happening crowd.'

Rishi didn't miss the suggestive blink that accompanied the mention of 'happening crowd'. He ignored it. Shabnam waited for him to ask more. When he didn't, she pointed to the cycle. 'Else, the only thing I can offer is this. Take it and go for a ride. When you are back, leave it in the clear patch of the eucalyptus forest.'

'What if it gets stolen?'

'No one other than you would steal this.' She giggled again. 'This is an old model; tyres go flat every other week. If someone does steal it, we will be one liability lighter.'

Rishi sat on the cycle and pedalled away. He rode through the beautiful campus of the Indian Institute of Advanced Studies on Cart Road. He rested the cycle against a tree and walked through the woods, whistled at the breathtaking gardens, and sat at the in-house coffee shop with a steaming cup of Americano, secretly wishing Shabnam would drop in, even if to just claim the cycle for some immediate need. Nothing like that happened. After an hour, as he rode back following the same path, he picked some primroses in violet, yellow and white and kept them in the cycle's basket. He parked it where he had been asked to.

When he got home, the Major was standing with a huge frown on his forehead, a binocular hanging from his neck. 'Whose cycle were you riding?'

'Are you trying to spy on me?' The peace treaty they had called the night before had vanished.

'I saw you riding a bicycle. It had some flowers in the basket,' he pronounced disapprovingly.

Rishi shrugged stubbornly. 'Well, I won't tell you.' He ran inside, leaving his uncle fuming.

Was the boy having an affair here in Shimla? He would now have to keep a keen eye on the boy to figure out whether he could at all be trusted with his daughter.

After lunch, when Rishi set out for a walk, he met Shabnam again a few miles from the house. She seemed to have come searching for him; and she was mad at him. They stood in an isolated part of the valley, guarded by sal trees from all sides.

'Are you nuts?' She made no attempt to disguise her anger. 'Why on earth did you put those flowers in my basket?'

Rishi didn't understand what had gone wrong. Didn't flowers make women happy any longer? 'I left those because I didn't have anything else to give you in return.' He said matter-of-factly.

'Oh, please!' Shabnam snapped at him. 'Reserve these give-and-takes for the plains downhill. Here, we don't expect a return for every little thing we do.'

'What's the problem, Shabnam?' Rishi asked, shocked at her sudden rudeness.

'Everyone is asking me who put those flowers in my basket, and why! I have no answer. My people won't understand that those flowers are harmless gratitude and nothing more. You understand now?' Shabnam blurted out the words, and found Rishi smiling.

'What?' she asked impatiently.

'Who said there wasn't anything more?' he braved.

Enraged, Shabnam tried to find appropriate words to call out this nonsense. She raised a finger at him. 'Stay away from me,' she said and walked away.

Rishi walked behind her. 'This is unfair, Shabbo,' he laughed.

'Don't you call me that!' Shabnam hissed. His amused face infuriated her even more. She picked up a pebble and threw it at him. It missed the target. Rishi laughed again. She chased him. He fled. She ran between the sal trees and stopped, gasping. Silence everywhere. Only a few birds chirruped from high up. The sound of her breath seemed to echo through the tall trees. He had disappeared. She tried to gauge where he was hiding. Stealthily, Rishi crept up from behind her, and with a sudden deft movement, opened the bun that held her hair tightly in place. They fell like waves across her shoulders and back. She spun around. Without giving him a moment to make an escape, she placed her leg at the back of his knees and pulled. He fell on the rough forest floor.

'Ouch!' he yelped. His hands and waist hurt. She looked down at him, fire in her eyes. 'What was that?' he exclaimed.

She didn't answer, neither did she make any attempt to help him up. Rishi hauled himself up, rubbing the bruised areas. She looked at those and then back at him.

'You know karate?' he asked.

'No,' she said. 'I am in the NCC.'

'But that doesn't change anything. I am hurt, but not scared.' Rishi started flirting again.

'Don't act smart,' Shabnam said angrily. 'I will walk up to the Major and spill your secret.'

'What destruction do you think that will bring? What further destruction? There's nothing that can go worse than today.' For a split second, the Major's rants flashed in his brain from the evening before. 'Go try it.' He rubbed his elbow.

Shabnam had forgotten to tie her hair back. They flew around her face with the breeze. Her dupatta lay carelessly on her body, no longer covering her head. She stood still, like a warrior woman, having defeated the disobedient with a stroke of her sword. To her utter disappointment, though, the vanquished still breathed. Rishi's eyes hovered over her. She turned to leave. He did not move an inch. A few steps away, she turned.

'Are you coming?'

'Only when you want me to,' he said suggestively.

'Rishi!' she said, frustrated. 'Please stop flirting. This is not for me. Please.'

'I am serious,' he admitted.

'I don't have time for this crap!' she frowned, ready to move on.

'Come when you are done with everything else. I shall wait.' She opened her mouth again, but Rishi didn't let her speak. 'Shhhh…' he gestured, putting a finger on his lips, and said softly, 'Guess we both have said what we had to. Now leave.'

She waited for a few more seconds, staring at the stubborn face in front. Then she walked off.

Late that night, Rishi lay on his bed, thinking about the afternoon. His phone rang. Mira. Remembering something important, he disconnected her call. He typed in a WhatsApp message and hit 'Send'. 'If you don't have anything to do with her, please leave her alone.' Pat came the reply, as if Viyaan was sitting with his phone in hand, waiting for a text from Rishi.

'I didn't have anything to do with her…till a few evenings back.'

After a few seconds, another message reached him. 'She's safe with me. Please stay out of this.'

Rishi smiled and dialled his sister back.

26.

'Are you seeing someone these days? Dad was telling me today that the boy's character is dicey.'

'Not seeing, really.'

'What do you mean, not really? There's someone? Tell me, you monster.'

'I just like someone. Nothing more. And it's one-sided.'

'One-sided? From the girl's end?'

'No. From my end.'

Mira didn't know how to react to that. Rishi! Her brother. Girls were charmed by him even without his trying! And there's some girl on this planet who wasn't interested in him when he was?

'Who?' she managed to ask.

'Shabnam.'

'Rishi!' Mira lost her voice again.

The brother didn't respond. Shabnam had crept into the deepest corners of his heart yet uninhabited and was now spreading like watercolour on a wet canvas. She was like a monarch who wouldn't adjust to fit into his frame. A woman beyond the scope of his camera.

'Rishi,' Mira repeated, bringing him back to their conversation. 'Shabnam is our gardener's daughter!'

'Shabnam is an IAS aspirant, Browny.' He was curt.

'Rishi,' Mira was almost shouting on the phone. 'Why do you do these things deliberately when you know it will irk your parents? Shabnam is…!' she stopped abruptly.

'Her father wouldn't have killed a snake before lying dead, had he considered on that morning what you just refrained from saying,' the brother uttered bitterly.

'It might get difficult for you. Stop, if you can,' the sister pleaded.

'Things aren't hunky-dory now either.'

'Even before one issue settles, you pick up another. How will it work? This way you will only let the misunderstandings grow.' Mira felt helpless.

'Don't worry, Browny. Shabnam and I aren't together. It could just end as a passing interest. We will talk, if at all it's meant to be.' He abruptly put an end to the discussion. 'What's happening with Iyer?'

'I didn't know he had a house in Bengaluru. He has called me there.' Mira's voice at the end of the sentence was almost inaudible.

'He was born and brought up there. You are going?'

'Shouldn't I?' she asked, wishing that her brother would say yes. Or no. Or something that she could adapt as her decision.

'I have heard that he has a big flat in Bengaluru. He stays there alone, with only servants for company, whenever he is in town.'

'Alone? He doesn't have a family?' Mira asked.

'No.' Rishi informed her. 'His parents divorced and remarried. Neither of them stays with him.'

For a few moments the cousins remained quiet. Mira broke the silence. 'I can't bring myself to say no to him. As much as

I decide otherwise, he convinces me. I don't know whether it is my curiosity or something else.'

'You are sorted, then.' The brother shrugged. 'Explore yourself. If you ever feel you don't want to proceed further, stop right there. And let me know. I'll get you back.'

Mira smiled. Her cousin always had only one solution to all her problems. He, himself.

'Listen carefully now, Browny,' he said. 'I have a plan. We only have a few more days with us. Let's get this cracking now.'

'Yes. High time. I think Deepti Bua is also prepared. She asks me about myself every day. Let's strike while the iron is hot,' Mira agreed.

'Let's write letters to the siblings. I will write to mom on behalf of the Major, and you write to him on behalf of my mother. The letters will have to be compelling enough, so they are left with no choice but to see each other urgently. We shall make them come face to face with each other and see how it goes from there. Sounds good?'

They hung up. Mira sat thinking. She looked at the phone again. With a frown on her forehead, she lifted it. Two missed calls from Viyaan. She dialled back.

In another two hours, Mira stood outside the flat in Malleswaram. She hesitated and then rang the bell. An old man opened the door. He said something in Tamil, of which she understood nothing. The flat had milky white walls done up in tasteful accessories. The pillars had wonderful motifs on them. No one needed to tell her who had designed those. The old man guided her through the living room, asked her to sit on the sofa, served her a glass of water and disappeared. When he left, Mira got up and looked around the room—large, wall-size glass doors that opened out to a terrace with pretty potted plants; huge paintings on the walls; lamps; a semicircular sofa; a centre table with decorative silver bowls on it; and an antique clock on the wall that must have been an inheritance. No photographs or portraits anywhere. She studied the wall in fascination.

'Hey' Viyaan's voice made her turn, only to turn back again, shocked. The man had just come out from a bath. He was still wiping his hair with a towel, wearing a pair of jeans and nothing on top. The black tattoos shone on his white skin. Embarrassed, Mira curled her toes against the floor. She felt unsteady. Even though she wasn't facing him, she could feel Viyaan's eyebrows coming together in a frown; she could tell when he threw the towel on one corner of a chair and walked towards her. She closed her eyes in denial.

'Turn, Mira,' he commanded from behind. She didn't move.

'You can't face away from me like this. It hurts. Please,' he said again.

'Wear something,' Mira fumbled. Her palms were sweating.

'I won't, till you have looked at me. I want you to see me. Properly. Turn.' She didn't. He held her by the shoulders and made her turn. He locked eyes with her, putting an end to all her resistance. He lifted her hand and made her touch the sun tattoo on his chest. Those once felt weird and scary, but today they seemed mysterious, magnetic and beautiful. Viyaan himself looked like an exquisite piece of sculpture, his body carved with razor-sharp tools to shape the jawline, the chest and the waist. She didn't realize when Viyaan let go of her hand and she was exploring his body by herself, running her fingers along his neck, the muscles on his shoulder, the strong line of his jaw.

'I am exactly eleven years older to you. Does that leave room for future regrets later?'

Lost in the drumming of her own heart, his deep, seductive voice felt like a caress. She wasn't her usual rational self and Viyaan's words eluded her comprehension. She looked on blankly, unable to take her eyes off him. A faint, naughty grin lit up his handsome features, as if he had his victim firmly trapped in the confines of his cave. 'I am leaving for London tonight for fifteen days. Conferences.'

This one made sense. It meant he'd not be around. But this piece of information did not bring her the relief she was expecting. Mira looked away, a strange uncertainty written on her face. Viyaan touched her neck softly, bringing her eyes back to him. 'Trust me, I am the best thing around you right now,' he whispered in her ears, craving to reserve the attention of those large eyes only for himself.

'When I am back, I will be in Mumbai, and you in Shimla. I need to seal something before we are off.'

He girdled her waist with his hands and pulled her closer. Mira felt a tremor in her legs.

'You know where this is heading, right?' Viyaan whispered affectionately, his mouth very close to hers. 'Stop me if you want. I'll understand.' She closed her eyes, too powerless to decide. He let out a hot breath of air; her face went red, her veins tensed. He waited, giving her time to push him away. Mira inched closer. He picked her up and sat her on a tall table. He looked up at her face, put a hand behind her head and pulled her down towards his mouth.

✳

Back from Malleswaram, Mira stood by the window. Her body still shivered from Viyaan's touch. The small of her back could still feel his hands. She felt Viyaan was still looking at her from some corner. As if he would hug her again, take her by surprise. Everything had happened so fast. She felt feverish. One kiss meant giving up something she had retained for twenty-four years of her life. She hadn't known what it felt like to be touched. She hadn't known that lips, too, had a mind of their own, which knew exactly what to do when the moment arrived. Being so close to Viyaan, letting go of her restraint, aligning their rhythms to the same beat, and believing whatever had happened was true, had left her in a daze.

A hand from behind brought her back to the present. Deepti Bua stood there, looking at her strangely.

'I have been calling you for so long. What have you been thinking?'

'Nothing, Ma'am, was just a little distracted.'

'All okay?' she asked anxiously.

'Yes. Actually, no.' She took the opportunity to test the waters. 'It's Mira. We keep talking about her every other day. It's about her.'

'What about her?' Deepti Bua looked at her with anxious eyes. 'What happened?'

'I am not sure. A common friend just said that something has happened to her family. She seemed very upset. She didn't talk to anyone in college.'

'Why? What's the matter?' Deepti Bua's voice had risen with growing impatience.

'I'm not sure. I asked the friend to find out and let me know.'

'You don't have her number?' Deepti Bua asked breathlessly, as if her heart threatened to jump out of her mouth any minute. Mira wanted to hug her and cry, but she steadied herself, looking away.

'I don't, Ma'am. Mira isn't a very smart girl. She doesn't talk to too many people. She isn't friendly. She responds, but can't converse. Her classmates make fun of her.'

'She is her father's daughter.' The words escaped her aunt before she could check them. Disturbed and worried, Deepti Bua went back inside. Mira watched her leaving, happy that the foundation for the plan's climax had been set.

Late in the night, she heard Deepti Bua talking to Sharat Uncle.

'Wait a moment, let me ask Akshat,' her husband said.

Mira sat up straight. It hadn't occurred to her that they could verify with Akshat Uncle. Quickly she dialled his number herself, but it was engaged. She kept her ears open to keep track of whatever was transpiring in the other room. The call began and ended cordially. Akshat Uncle must have said that he would find out and let them know. She breathed a sigh of relief. Akshat Uncle needed to be kept in the loop about everything they did now. Else things could turn out to be a disaster. She must tell Rishi.

She let her body fall back on the bed. Her mind went back to where it had been hovering all through the day. He had sent her a text when he had boarded the flight.

That morning when Mira had sat inside Viyaan's car, he had suddenly asked, 'Who is Shayan Chatterjee?'

Hearing the name so suddenly from him, Mira faltered. 'My....mmm...well, no...actually...our professor. My thesis guide. My intern…I mean, I am an intern under him…Yes!' she said, looking outside the window.

'You have a crush on him?'

'No. Of course not. Not at all.'

'Yes.'

'No.'

'You are blushing. And you're stammering again. It's a yes, 100 per cent!'

'Stop!' Mira looked outside the window to save herself from Viyaan's wolf eyes.

'I know half the professors in your college. I will find out about him,' Viyaan had said indifferently, starting the car.

'No!' Mira was terrified about this possibility.

He gave her a mischievous grin. 'Gotcha! Stay warned of your ways, girl, else you will invite trouble.'

Little nothings, still too fresh in her mind and body, kept her awake almost till morning.

27.

Rishi entered through the gate of the bungalow when the sun had set and it was slowly getting dark. At the entrance, just beside the gulmohar tree, he found a cycle standing. Shabnam's. Quickly he walked behind the tree and stood on tiptoe to look inside. There she was, talking to the Major very seriously. In a short while, he found her coming out of the house. He stood still. When she came for her cycle, she found Rishi standing under the tree with hands crossed across his chest and eyes narrowed at her. She dragged him by the arm to a corner where no one would see them.

'Whoaaaaaahhhh, hold on! Well, this was unexpected,' he chuckled.

'Shut up.' Shabnam looked around and whispered, 'Major Sahab thinks you are Mira Didi's boyfriend. He thinks Mira Didi sent you here, so you could come to terms with her dad. And he thinks you are two-timing with me.'

Appalled, Rishi was about to shout out a curse, but Shabnam gestured to him to keep quiet.

'I told him that I have nothing to do with any of it. Now you settle things your way. I should not be dragged into this any further, you understand?' she warned.

The initial shock gone, Rishi started laughing. She frowned. 'What?'

'This is why he has been after my life all this while? Such meaningless inferences!' He looked at the house. 'Now watch how I take revenge on him. He gave away my favourite orange T-shirt to the watchman. It's my turn now.' He let out a dramatic toot to announce the start of an unspoken war.

'Rishi,' Shabnam told him as she left. 'Don't trouble him.'

He winked. 'Just wait and watch.' He smiled and strode off. Shabnam shook her head and rode out of the main gate.

Late that night, Rishi approached the Major asking for permission to use the desktop set up in his room. 'My laptop has some issues,' he said. He switched on the computer. When the Major wasn't looking, he took out his pen drive and transferred some photographs to the computer. Those were some of his childhood images with Mira.

'What's this?' he shouted suddenly. 'What the hell is this?'

Surprised with this sudden rise in decibel, the Major left his whisky and came to check what was bothering the boy so much. 'What?' he asked, irritated.

Rishi lowered his voice. 'Your daughter had a childhood sweetheart?' He tried to keep his face unflickeringly serious.

'What?' the Major was outraged. 'What did you just say?'

'Look.' He flashed the images on the screen. 'What are these?'

The Major stared at them longer than usual. Two beautiful children hugging, smiling, playing and running around the lawn stared back at him. He turned to Rishi, with a deep trench between his eyebrows. 'What's your problem?'

'Your daughter always says that she misses someone from her childhood. She never told me it was a boy. Now I understand what she'd been trying to hint at all this while! I don't believe this.' He looked incredulous.

The Major looked at him as if he would slap him hard. He just went back to his seat and fell back into it, resigned. Rishi hastily rose from the chair and went to stand beside him. His uncle stared at the ground for a long time. 'Mira never had a friend, let alone a boyfriend. The photographs you just saw are those of her cousin.' He sounded miserable. Rishi felt sorry for him.

'Mira's brother? Your nephew? Where is he now?'

'Last I heard, they were in Bengaluru. After that I don't know,' he admitted sadly.

'You don't know? Your sister, your nephew, and you don't know? Then who knows?' he charged. The Major didn't have an answer. Rishi softened his voice. 'Don't you miss them? Don't you feel like knowing where they are, how they are, what they are doing? Didn't you ever wonder how this boy looks, now that he must have grown up?' Agony had crept into Rishi's voice, but thankfully, the Major wasn't in a state to detect the sudden change in tone. Rishi had started pouring out the allegations he had against his uncle, all in third person. But the anguish was as genuine as his questions. He looked at his uncle, willing him to answer. The uncle kept staring at the ground.

'My sister and I had a bitter fight. After that she never came back. Neither did I go to her. Every day I tell myself that I should. But I can't convince myself to pick up the phone and make that call.' He got up and tried to make his way to the minibar. Rishi blocked his path.

'You won't do this today. You will not hide behind another peg of whisky, seeking this temporary relief from your conscience. Face it yourself.'

The Major didn't speak, but Rishi couldn't bring himself to stop. 'You have spoilt the childhood of two children. Look at them. See how happy they were with each other. What have you done, Major Sahab?' he blurted out. The Major covered his face with his hands.

Rishi knew this man wouldn't sleep tonight. He passed him a glass of water. The Major didn't ask him to leave. Rishi sat through the night on the chair in front of the computer, pretending to work, as the Major constantly changed sides on his bed. At the end of the night, with the mind heavily spent, he fell asleep. The nephew pulled a blanket over him and left the room.

Some sentiments are personal. They are deep and impassioned. They expose the raw, unfabricated feelings of the heart so ruthlessly that it feels naked. As Rishi walked down the balcony under the galaxy of glittering stars, he could almost hear the sighs and groans of the old house, having found an escape after years of solitary imprisonment.

The next morning when the Major woke up, he found Rishi standing on his balcony. For a few seconds, it felt nostalgic. His balcony faced the flower beds in the garden. As children, his daughter and nephew would get together on his balcony early in the mornings to watch Shiraz work, till the front door was opened and they were free to run outside. After Deepti left, many times he had found Mira standing there alone, looking down at the garden. She never asked him questions. She never accused him of spoiling her childhood and drowning her in frustrating isolation. She never even asked him to bring them back. His little daughter had given him the repose that only humanity could bring. It was called acceptance.

The guilt made him more introverted than he already was. But even the enormous strength of his body could not convince the weak mind that it was perhaps time to go back. Forsaken by his only sister, he had harboured the pain of loss deep within himself all these years. Sometimes answers came only when questions were asked; and forgiveness demanded conditions to be met. But that, again, was a personal space that no one could touch or heal; not even time.

The Major got up and walked to the balcony to stand beside Rishi. He put a hand on his shoulder.

'You didn't sleep?'

The boy shook his head.

'Why?' he asked, despite knowing the answer. Last night had been confession time. No one had ever seen the Major falling so weak. But it had also broken some barriers between the two.

Rishi didn't answer. He just smiled at the Major and looked away. What he appreciated about his uncle was that last evening, Rishi was not grilled about Shabnam. He suspected Rishi to be two-timing, but the fact that one of them was his own daughter and the other his gardener's didn't bother him. At least one person in his life wasn't prejudiced. Driven by an overwhelming surge of emotions that kept him awake through the night, he, on an impulse, threw himself at the Major and hugged him tight. This time he wasn't pushed away. The Major hugged him back.

*

That afternoon he went back to the sal forest. He sat there alone, thinking about the way things were scattered now. The cousins were only a few steps away from their destination. This had to reach its deserving climax. Rishi looked out at nothing. Soon a prank floated into his mind like a boat, gently sailing through calm waters but sending out gigantic ripples. This was it! Eyes twinkled, hands tapped a beat, lips smiled. Coming up soon was his sweetest revenge on his uncle and his mother. He opened a file carrying hand-written documents by the Major. He studied his handwriting minutely. Next, he pulled out a paper to write a letter to his mother. He signed it as Major General Anil Dhillon. The only job left now was to get this couriered.

He looked up. A little distance away, Shabnam was riding her bicycle, neatly folded clothes strapped on to the pillion seat. Perhaps she was out for a delivery. His eyes followed her as long as she was in range. He quietly got up, pulled out a piece of chalk from his pocket and wrote his phone number on a sal tree.

That evening when he went back, he found it wiped clean, perhaps with a few leaves or a piece of cloth. And water.

28.

Mira could sense how unsettled Deepti Bua had been since she had heard that there was something wrong at Major Dhillon's house. She had made a call to Akshat Uncle again. This time there was no mistake. Akshat Uncle confirmed that something indeed was wrong but he didn't yet know what it was. Deepti Bua had been even more restless since. Sharat Uncle had tried to engage her in an English-versus-Physics debate, but that hadn't worked. She had been walking aimlessly around the house, talking to herself, unmindful of everything she was doing. She prayed in the little temple in her room ten times in the day. Utensils fell from her distracted hands. Frequently, she forgot things that she had said, having transformed into a bundle of nerves.

At night, after she slept, Sharat Uncle sat down with Mira to unwind.

'You have no idea what peculiar characters they are. Both brother and sister. Impulsive that she is, Deepti blamed Anil for not giving enough time to his wife, especially during her last few days. I advised her not to go there, but Deepti is Deepti. In his heart, Anil, too, had started blaming himself. One day he couldn't take the pressure any longer and burst out, trying to defend himself. He ended up being as unpleasant as he could be to his only sister.'

Lost in a difficult stretch of the past, Sharat Bahl didn't notice Mira weeping silently. Neither she, nor Rishi was ever told the genesis of the fight between the siblings.

She silently wiped her tears with her hands, as Sharat Uncle spoke again. 'They never forgave each other; they never went back. They fell prey to an ego that didn't give them any peace in return for the beautiful togetherness it took away. I tried to mediate, but it didn't work. Both of them are high-headed people,' he said sadly.

'Not forgive each other,' Mira wondered. 'They needed to forgive themselves.' Her father needed to heal. He needed care. So did her bua.

'Initially, I would speak to him often. Anil was as warm with me as he had always been. I kept him informed of everything that was happening with us. He listened, at times offered his inputs too. But whenever I tried to discuss Deepti, he grew silent. And as it happens, a one-sided attempt can't last long. My calls to him started getting fewer and eventually I stopped altogether. Anil didn't ask why. Perhaps he thought it was an extended repercussion of what had happened between him and his sister.' Sharat Uncle nodded absently. 'Strange it is.'

He looked outside at the dark silhouettes of the coconut trees, their crowns swaying in the breeze. 'Deepti, Anil and I were friends. We had lots of fun together. We were inseparable, though we came from different disciplines. I from English, Deepti from Physics and Anil from Economics.' He covered his face with his palms, remembering the beautiful times they had left behind. 'We had lunch together, sat talking for hours, played cricket and tennis. He was always a little shy, a little introverted, and I used to be the pulse of the college. Sometimes

Akshat would come along; he was Deepti's classmate. When Anil joined the Army and was going through rigorous training, there were times when he wanted to give up and come back. Those days Deepti and her parents requested me to give him pep talks. I convinced him to hold on, to just let the phase pass. And he got through.'

He relaxed, coming back to the present. 'A lot changes after marriage, and it's not just between spouses. With whatever transpired between Anil and Deepti, I was rendered useless. Anil never opened up to me the way he used to. From being a friend, I had suddenly become his sister's husband, which demanded that a formal distance be maintained. There were facts to be hidden, suppressed and avoided. That's society! He didn't allow me to help this time.'

'What about Ma'am?' Mira asked softly.

'Deepti…' Sharat Uncle looked defeated. 'Deepti tries to show that she is very strong and always in control. But she is actually the weakest among us. Dominating enough to impose but not secure enough to apologize. Her brother's words that morning left her shaken. She was charming once. Rigid but cheerful. Now her insecurity shows as impatience, especially with her son.'

Even after Sharat Uncle left, Mira couldn't sleep. She looked out of the window. The flickering street lights placed at regular intervals inside the society didn't illuminate much. They only darkened further all those areas they couldn't reach, one of them being her mind.

Could she and Rishi ever separate after a fight, like their parents had? Would she ever behave like her father? She shuddered at the thought.

No! She dismissed the thought immediately.

Really? Another part of her brain raised its cynical head. *Then what kept you from sending that friend request to Rishi over Facebook, when you were already checking his profile three times a day?*

He didn't either.

That's the point. Reluctance to take the first step as a guard against possible humiliation.

Problem No. 3,267: Returns? Reciprocations? Or just love?

She thought of the other side of the coin. *What about Rishi? Why didn't he ever make an attempt all those years?* She found that answer too. He was probably not even thinking about her. He wasn't one to spend time debating whether or not to go ahead with something. He wasn't scared of repercussions. Rishi always prioritized life with whatever was available. He didn't chase goals; he only enhanced his skills and created assets. Goals happened to him!

Mira stood there alone, trying to pick up the fallen pieces of her life and put them back together in her head. Her father and aunt seemed different personalities now, people she had only half-known all these years.

Quietly she went back to her writing table.

Dear Bhai,

It's been sixteen long years. So much for believing that one day you would just pick up the phone and call. Maybe you thought the same.

I am writing this letter because I am scared to call. What if you slam the phone down on my face and refuse to talk? But it is important that I tell you something, which I might not be able to later.

*I am unwell, Bhai. No one other than Sharat knows, not even
Akshat. Please don't tell him anything. Before it's too late, I want
to see you once. Please come.*
Deepti

She finalized this after tearing off the first seven attempts. Mira
couldn't convince herself that she was writing something so
stupid. But Rishi had said it had to be compelling enough. So
there it was. She placed it inside an envelope and put it inside
her bag, to be posted early in the morning.

The next day started with the usual banter between Sharat Uncle
and Deepti Bua. Mira stopped brushing and tried to catch the
conversation.

'Come on, Deepti. Why are you so bothered about him if
he hasn't cared for all these years? Move on, lady,' Sharat Uncle
was telling her. 'Think about how many times Anil has betrayed
you. He made promises which he didn't fulfil. I don't think he
deserves so much attention.'

'Can't you just keep quiet? Why do you have to talk so
much?' Deepti Bua tried to snap him off.

Mira chuckled. Sharat Uncle was trying reverse psychology.
This could be interesting. She heard him speak again.

'Look, Deepti. I never said this before, but today I must say
that Anil has let you down in more ways than one. Remember
he didn't come for your convocation because of his NDA
entrance examinations? And then, even for our wedding, he
appeared at the last moment, like a guest. Remember how he
shouted when you had accidentally burnt his uniform? You were

only trying to help, ironing out the creases. When Rishi was born, he didn't even come to see him. He came only when his holidays started. Such an opportunist!'

That was enough. Deepti Bua now erupted at him. 'What the hell are you saying? Have you lost your mind? My brother has spent his life serving the country! He has been sent to weird places, with the strangest people. He has stayed without food and water. He hasn't compromised on his duties ever. He is with the Army, Sharat! Not in a stupid government office where you can take liberties at your whims!'

'You just said it.' Sharat Uncle left his wife stumped with that and moved away.

It was late in the afternoon when the courier boy delivered an envelope. Deepti Bua opened it and frowned for a very long time. When she had finished reading it, her expression had changed. She seemed angry enough to slaughter anyone who came in front of her. Sharat Uncle and Mira looked at her, unable to comprehend what had gone wrong.

'I don't believe this. I just don't believe this.' She was breathing heavily. Mira ran towards her with a glass of water. Sharat Uncle rushed to her too, asking incessantly what had happened.

Deepti Bua handed him the piece of paper.

Deepti,
I hope you are fine. You have always led a fine life, so there's no reason why you shouldn't be. But here I have to tell you something important.

I have fallen in love with an Australian tourist called Chloe. She is a journalist and a student of literature. She is completely taken with the photographs I have clicked and my collection of cameras. Soon she wants to host an exhibition in Australia and get a book published on those. Given her contact in the media there, my long-term hobby will finally find its due.

I have already put in my papers. I want to marry Chloe by the end of next month.

The only problem is, Mira doesn't understand this. She shouts and cries. Now she will be married off soon. So she won't necessarily stay with her stepmom. I tried to explain things to her, but she says she wants to go and stay with you. My only request, please come and help out. First, be a witness to my wedding. Next, either explain it to Mira or take her with you for a few days. I will settle things in Australia and come back for her.

Hope you won't disappoint.
Anil

Both Sharat Uncle and Deepti Bua seemed stunned. The letter didn't leave them in a position to check on Mira. Else they would have found her fuming. Sharat Uncle read it again.

'So this is what he has been doing for sixteen years! That's why he never called me. I would have been a hindrance.' Deepti Bua clenched her teeth. 'Now I know.'

Sharat Uncle still frowned. 'I find it weird.'

'What weird?' Deepti Bua yelled. 'You know his fascination for those cameras and photographs. Someone has just shown some interest in them and he has started thinking they are masterpieces.' She fumed. 'And Mira! My poor child. She is getting dragged into this mess! He has lost all virtue and discipline, planning a wedding with a girl who's half his age! Now he also wants Mira to be sent off soon, so that he can enjoy with his new bride. He has gone mad. He needs psychiatric treatment, and that…what is the name? Whatever… that Australian needs to be sent packing!'

Mira quietly slid away. Just before she entered her room, she heard Sharat Uncle say, 'How do you pronounce Chloe?'

'Oh! So now you are interested in *that*?' Deepti Bua lashed out at him. He tried to defend himself. Even in her rage, Mira couldn't help giggling. This boy, her cousin, needed to be whipped.

She heard Deepti Bua speaking again. 'Let's go. Tomorrow. Yes, tomorrow itself. I don't want to delay this any further. Sharat, please book the tickets.'

'What do we do with Sita? Her holidays are yet to get over,' he asked.

Deepti Bua got up from her seat. 'We will drop her at Akshat's place in Delhi. He will escort her back home. I am sure Sita will understand. We will bring her back again sometime. You explain it to her. I am going to pack my bags. I will pack some stones and daggers too, to throw at that Australian.'

'Chloe,' Sharat Uncle reminded her.

'Oh, shut up, Sharat! This is not the time for jokes. You talk to Sita.' She rushed inside.

Mira had started packing too, happy at the possibility of having the family back in Shimla. She was lost in her own world, when Sharat Uncle called her name softly from behind. 'Mira.'

Startled, she got up. He came forward and hugged her.

'I suspected right on the first day I saw you. But I wasn't sure. But this letter today could not have been written by anyone other than my nitwit son. These pranks are his identity.' He laughed with one hand on his belly, the other wiping the tears off his eye. 'The letter is stamped in Shimla. So I know what ruckus he is creating in Anil's life now. Poor guy, I pity him.'

Both Mira and Sharat Uncle broke into silent laughter.

'But let me tell you, that was pure genius.' He winked and rushed back to the other room, from where Deepti Bua had just called him for help.

29.

Shabnam got up early on Fridays. She offered her morning prayers and rode her bicycle towards the graveyard. She sat near her father's grave in silence, giving him an account of things. Her studies, her mother, the family, college, friends, life in Delhi, holidays in Shimla, and everything else. In the solitude of the place, he spoke back to her. Or so she felt.

This morning too, she let her cycle stand outside the rusty gate and stepped into the land where many lay peacefully in their eternal sleep. At a distance from the grave, though, she came to an abrupt halt. Her heart skipped several beats. Without making a noise, she walked on and stood behind a pine. Rishi was leaning against a tree, singing a song that could wake up the dead. Her father's favourite song. His music navigated the chords exactly like her father's had, touching each note, each lyric, with great affection, pausing at the same beats and catching his breath in a way that was engraved in her heart as her father's distinct identity. She clasped the trunk in front, watching him, her eyes heavy with the flood of memories. The veil on her head slipped off with the breeze; she didn't notice. Unblinkingly, she stared ahead. The insides of her throat froze into a rigid lump. Her heart ached.

The melody of the song echoed between the graveyard and the pine trees, even when Rishi had stopped. He sat there aimlessly, in no hurry to leave. The breeze dropped some dry leaves from the plants above, their rustles and murmurs disturbing the sombre quiet of the place. He inched towards the grave. Anxious, Shabnam stepped backwards to ensure she was hidden from his view. He touched the surface of the grave and brushed away the fallen leaves. Gently, he moved his fingers over the stone as if he were touching the skin of her father. As if he were communicating something personal and obscure, stopping to listen from him and humming again, to exchange some undisclosed information carefully kept secret from the rest of the world.

The tears felt wet against her cheeks. Shabnam quickly pressed her palm to her mouth and rushed out of the graveyard. Once in a silent, secluded place, she let herself fall on the thin grass and wept. She hadn't cried when her father had died; she had just held her devastated mother as tight as she could and stared at the lifeless body of her father in disbelief. Today, years later, the unexpressed grief had found its release.

It was midday when Rishi returned from his walk. At the gate, the courier boy was delivering an envelope. Saundarya Ma accepted it and looked at it with a frown. Then, hastily, she went inside. Rishi ran after her.

'Major Sahab, it's from Bengaluru,' she said, panting. The book that he was reading dropped from his hands.

'Bengaluru?' He looked up at her, startled. Confusion written all over his face, he received the envelope. He ran his fingers on the space where his name and address had been written in ink. His sister seemed to have changed her mind. Finally, a letter from Bengaluru. He took a deep breath, as if still coming to terms with the fact that it had indeed come from a place that had been silent for so long. When he opened his mouth, he said something that made Rishi chuckle from behind the door. Saundarya grunted in frustration.

'Now I know why Mira's grammar and spellings are so bad,' he complained. 'It's in her blood, it's come from her bua! There are errors here, right on the envelope. She is so careless. Even reading this handwriting is such a pain. But you tell her this, and she will flare up.'

'Major Sahab, can you just open the envelope and read what is written inside? You have received a letter after sixteen years, and all you are talking about is bad handwriting?' Saundarya couldn't hold herself back.

The Major didn't seem to be in any hurry. Perhaps he wanted to prolong the experience. He looked at the envelope and ran his fingers along it for a while longer before finally breaking open the seal. Rishi could see that behind the apparent calm, his uncle was tense. Once he had the piece of paper in his hands, he opened the folds and started reading. Lines of deep concern appeared on his face.

By the time he had finished, he looked broken. He gulped down a glass of water. Up and down the room he paced, trying to cool his strained nerves. It didn't help. He tried to pick up his phone and dial Akshat. His number was not reachable. Saundarya kept asking what was wrong, but he didn't answer. He tried to call and speak to Mira, but her phone was switched off. Frustrated, he threw the phone on the ground. Before it could hit the concrete and break into pieces, Rishi caught it from behind. No one complimented him on the brilliant catch.

He picked up the piece of paper on the table. No one stopped him. He read till the end and kept it back. 'The ever-sentimental Mira. Couldn't think of something more creative than this.' He looked up to find Saundarya waiting earnestly to be told whatever was brewing. He explained in brief.

She started crying. 'Why did you two stay away from each other for so many years, Major Sahab? I am a small person... what right do I have interfering in the family's personal matters? But when one person is stubborn, the other has to stoop and make it easy. What is the point of dragging one day for an entire lifetime? I agree that women should be demure and obedient, but what's the harm if men also try to understand? Poor Deepti Di.' She wiped her tears.

Her reactions felt unsettling. Rishi wanted to tell her that his mom wasn't dying and that she could relax. But, of course, he couldn't. He concentrated on his uncle instead, who looked shattered.

'Do you feel that the argument you had with your sister is any longer important, Sir?' Rishi asked softly. 'One day life will pull you apart anyway. Why do you need to do with someone you love what life does mercilessly in its own time? Help yourself, Sir. Go and get her back.'

Rishi seemed to be saying the same things to himself. It had been ages that he had spoken to his mother properly. The letter Mira had sent and Saundarya's tears had touched a nerve with him too. What if this were true? What if there was no more time to rebuild everything they had wasted? People misbehave with their loved ones, they take them for granted, because they believe in a tomorrow when things will get sorted. But what if there was no tomorrow? Today, right now, things had to be mended. Else, the casual distance you created today might never be forgiven by life. Eventually, it will play the same card to separate you permanently from each other.

'I will leave for Bengaluru right now,' the Major said and rushed out of the room. Just then, a car honked at the gate. Saundarya went to the balcony to see who it was. Two seconds of silence. And then almost immediately she was running downstairs, laughing, crying and saying something in Tamil all at the same time. She ran through the path downstairs and stopped only when she had hugged the elderly lady standing at the gate.

Deepti Bahl patted her back. 'Don't cry, Saundarya. Don't worry. Now that I am here, everything will be fine. No one can mess with Mira.'

Not sure about what she had just heard, Saundarya had her own pent-up emotions to release. 'You have done the right thing, Didi, by coming here. I will take care of you now. You should have come much earlier. Who holds grudges against their own brother? Women shouldn't have so much of resentment in their hearts. See how nature has punished you.' She wiped her eyes with the corner of her sari. 'Now that you are here, you will be absolutely fine.'

'Yes,' Rishi heard his mother agreeing. 'Now that I am here, there will be no other blunder. Mira will be absolutely fine. Just let me meet the aspiring groom once, and I will fix his brain right away.'

Before Saundarya could react, Major General Dhillon came rushing down the stairs. He stopped short at the sight of his sister. Deepti's anger and irritation evaporated as she looked at her brother through her horn-rimmed glasses. Neither of them spoke—they couldn't. It was Sharat Bahl who broke the silence, as he stepped forward and hugged his brother-in-law. They remained like that, tightly embracing each other for a few seconds. When they were done, the Major walked a few steps towards his sister. He placed a hand on her head.

'Deepti...' was all he managed to say.

Her eyes misted over, but she didn't take much time to come to the point either. 'Bhai, have you lost it? What's wrong with you?'

'I am okay. But you don't worry. Nothing will happen to you. I will...!'

The sister cut him short. 'What on earth will happen to me? But what's all this? Where the hell is this Clo? I shall throw her out of the house right now.'

After so many years, the Major wasn't expecting to be greeted like this. Neither did her words make any sense to him. He just looked on blankly, unable to think of a fitting response to these incomprehensible words. Sharat spoke before he did.

'Not Clo. It's Chloe. Chloe. You have to nicely round your mouth at the end to pronounce it properly,' he insisted. His wife ignored him.

Major General Dhillon didn't understand a word. 'What Clo?' he asked, flabbergasted.

Sharat butted in again. 'Chloe. Not Clo.'

Rishi fell to his knees at the corner of the stairs from where he had been watching the scene unfold. He laughed hysterically and his lungs threatened to burst.

The confusion downstairs continued for a while. The Major was shown the letter that had reached Bengaluru. He shrieked, gesticulating wildly, and stomped his feet to explain that this must have been a pathetic joke played by someone. He wasn't getting married, Mira's life was not getting messed up and there wasn't any Australian called Chloe who was holding an exhibition for him anywhere in the world. He, on his part, pulled out the letter from Bengaluru and showed it to his sister, which she dismissed in no time.

Discussions began in full vigour about who could have been the prankster, and the family started walking inside. Rishi got up and fled. He went to his room and bolted the door. He heard them pass through the corridor. Thankfully, with so much happening all of a sudden, the Major and Saundarya had forgotten all about him. When they were settled happily in the Major's room, catching up on life, he came out and stealthily stood outside their door to eavesdrop on the conversation.

'What's happening with Mira?' his mother asked.

The Major proudly told her about this new boy, Rahul Pandey, whom his daughter had very intelligently sent to his place so that he could get used to him, and vice versa. Rishi covered his mouth, lest he laugh out loud. He heard Sharat Bahl asking how the Major realized that Rahul Pandey was indeed Mira's suitor. He was told that Sunny had put it across to him one night.

'Sunny! Duffer!' Rishi wanted to punch him. He heard his father laughing, a little too much. The Major raised his voice to call Sunny and passed him some instructions. The very next moment, Rishi found himself being dragged into the room by the moron cook. Even though he resisted, Sunny pushed him inside. Rishi stood there sheepishly, looking at the ground, unwilling to look into his mother's eyes.

The lady stood up from her chair.

'This is Rahul Pandey?' she asked her brother. He nodded.

'You think he is Mira's suitor?' she asked again. He nodded again.

'Am I living in a world of crooks?' she shouted, sending her brother into shock again and her husband into splits. 'This is the idiot I gave birth to, Bhai! We don't need any explanation now as to who must have sent those letters to our houses.' She touched the tips of her fingers to her temples, as if trying to match all the things that had gone haphazard in the past one hour. The Major now got up to stand in front of Rishi. The nephew thought he would be slapped. He was hugged instead, affectionate hands patting him on the back and the head. He hugged his uncle. Today, finally, he had got his uncle back.

Their emotions were interrupted by a honk outside the gate once again. Everyone looked up, wondering if the day had any more surprises to throw up. They looked at Rishi, expecting him to have an answer.

'I think it's Mira. I'll get her,' he said and left. In a few seconds, Mira entered the room with Akshat Tiwari. Deepti Bahl stood up from her chair and then fell back into it again. Her eyes had tears in them. Mira touched their feet. The aunt held her by both hands.

'Why didn't you tell me when we dropped you at Delhi? You could have come with us!' she exclaimed.

Akshat smiled at her. 'Each story has its own climax, Deepti. No one is allowed to play a spoiler.'

They hugged, and laughed, and talked, and shouted, and abused, and laughed again. After lunch they all sat in the garden, talking about their good old days, catching up on whatever they had missed out all these years. Mira produced a big cardboard packet and kept it in front of her father.

'Dad,' she said. 'Rishi made this one for you.'

Everyone looked at each other. The Major removed the cover impatiently. Rishi's *Illusions* stared back at him. It took everyone in the room by awe. Sharat Bahl looked at his wife. She examined the frame carefully, running her hands over the printed face of her son and her brother. Speechless, the Major stared at it for a long time. Then he clasped Rishi's palm into his own and shook vigorously. Slowly, Mira said, 'They were ready to pay one and a half lakh for this frame. Rishi refused to sell it.'

A murmur of admiration and astonishment went around the group. While they praised Rishi, a look was exchanged between mother and son. Still stubborn, but pride glowing on her face, Deepti pouted and looked away. Rishi smiled.

Late that night, Rishi and Mira stood on the balcony, listening to Saundarya and Sunny arguing downstairs. They both claimed to know right from the beginning who Rahul Pandey had really been, but insisted they had kept quiet only to witness wisely the flow of events ahead. They both agreed that the other was lying.

'Should I tell them who Mira's real boyfriend is?' Rishi teased.

She winked. 'Sharat Uncle knows.'

'Really?' he frowned at her. 'Not surprising, though. People do grow bold when they are with Viyaan Iyer.'

She tried to slap him. He dodged her and went at her

from the side. She stumbled a few steps and pushed him back.

'If not anyone else, Saundarya Ma will be very happy,' he laughed. 'The real man is the Iyer man.' He imitated her accent. Mira laughed too. Her cell phone buzzed with a notification. Before she could get her phone, Rishi picked it up. There was a GIF on WhatsApp! Mushy kisses. In half a second, a thousand questions weeded into his brain.

Did they...? Did he...? To what extent...? How serious was this? Viyaan and Mira were from worlds apart. What if one of them couldn't sustain the relationship? Viyaan would move on easily, but what about his sister?

He wanted to punch Viyaan in the face. Almost immediately, he remembered, Viyaan was his boss. And that he was being the possessive, dominating brother again. His brain had gone on overdrive, but Mira snatched her phone back, checked her WhatsApp and giggled shyly. She looked at her brother and sobered up again, keeping the phone away.

The anxiety on Rishi's face was still evident. 'Tell me everything,' he demanded.

'Buzz off.' Mira tried to run but something Rishi said made her turn immediately.

'Hey, where has your diary reached? The one where you count your list of problems. Does Iyer know that he could be Problem No. 8,162 in one of its pages?'

Conscious and angry, she looked at Rishi. 'You read my diary!'

He grinned, showing his teeth.

'You cheat! Hopeless creature! It's my personal diary. How dare you!'

'Tell me everything; else I will tell Iyer that half your

problems in that funny book are because of him,' Rishi threatened, still laughing. But Mira suddenly remembered something, and her expression changed. Undaunted by his threats, she held out a piece of paper wordlessly and swayed it in front of him.

'What's that?' Rishi straightened up, the grin on its way out.

'Shabnam went back to Delhi this morning. She was at the gate when I arrived with Akshat Uncle. She handed this over to me.' Mira smiled mischievously.

Rishi's eyes narrowed; a shy glint appeared in them. He tried to snatch the piece of paper from her. She skipped back two steps. He ran towards her; she fled, with him chasing after her. Finally, under the gulmohar tree in the garden, he managed to catch hold of her. In the soft illumination of the gate lights, Rishi unfolded the piece of paper. Mira peeped in from the sides. He pushed her away.

The paper had no names—neither the receiver's, nor the sender's. Just a few digits. Rishi slipped the paper into his pocket.

'What has she written?' Mira asked shamelessly.

'Phone number.' Rishi winked.

'Shabnam's number?' She looked on.

'No, Virat Kohli's!' Rishi gave her a tap on the head.

Saundarya's voice shot up again from inside. Sunny had been watching Sunny Deol's action film on full blast when it was time for her Sun TV!

Acknowledgements

I get all my stories from a face that inspires me immensely. Shiraz, the character I loved creating the most, came from there. I start with thanking him first.

Rudra Narayan Sharma, Ujjaini Dasgupta, Elina Majumdar, Kapish Mehra—the entire team at Rupa Publications—much thanks for believing in *Summer Holidays*. A special note of thanks goes out to Shambhu Sahu for helping the manuscript transit from the author's desk to the publisher's, and for helping out with feedback every time I needed it.

Thanks to my entire family for being an unpredictable balance of chaos and calm. Biharis have their own quirks and Bengalis their own. My husband, Tuhin, and I have decided to keep those coming. Thanks to my parents, Ratna Dasgupta and D.R. Dasgupta, and my parents-in-law, Samira Sinha and Amarendra Kumar, for giving us the humour to do so.

Thanks to my cousins, whose contribution to my childhood memories is priceless—we still gang up against whoever is available.

Ranjan Pant, thanks for being the shield to my antics always, and for telling me that the men in my manuscripts need to behave!

Thanks to Sameer Desai and my college senior, Prodipta Roy, for sharing their inputs. Srushti Rao, I am immensely

thankful to you for showing me around Pearl Academy, an art
college in Mumbai. Swati Sharma, thanks for throwing light
on various aspects of being a local resident of Shimla. Thanks
to Varun Mehta and Dibyendu Chatterjee from IIT Bombay
for their time, the coffee and for not laughing when some of
my questions during the research phase were outrightly naive.

Dear readers, your mails and reviews keep me on my toes.
Your verdict is my reward. A big bow to you.

Neev Tanish, if there is one partner-in-comedy I can boast
of, it's you!

Aniruddha Sengupta, I still miss you…I still celebrate you.